Autobiography of Joker So Far

JACOB HERIC

A **True Joker Company** Publication

Portland, ME USA

www.truejokercompany.com

ISBN: 0692539506
True Joker Company ISBN: 978-0692539507

For Cass

PRAISE for *JOKER*:

"*JOKER* is a sweet, innocent and loveable young man. He is charming enough that you can usually forgive him for his annoying behavior and grating mannerisms."
-- Jane Kare, Assistant Town Clerk, CNP

"*JOKER* is a mixed up kid in the thrall of the Devil. However, he works hard and has a good attitude and, most importantly, he makes our blessed son laugh. For that we are thankful."
-- Humboldt Holton, NHRA (National Hardware Retail Assoc.)

"*JOKER* is one of a kind. Though his voice is rough and unconventional, you will not soon find a clearer or more poignant accounting of our time and place."
-- Mrs. Nancy Haberkorn, NTA (National Tutoring Assoc.) Regional Coordinator

"*JOKER* is a plucky, endearing adolescent. He is earnest, original, jovial and possesses an uncannily accurate perception of his social circumstances. Despite this, I'm afraid he is altogether not likely to amount to Prentice material."

-- Hamilcar Hernandez, Esq.

ACKNOWLEDGMENTS

Thanks Amy, Kurt and Hugh. Without your help this would be a complete mess. To the extent that it is still a mess, let us blame that on me, or better yet, let us claim that it is intentionally so. Thanks Rosa and May, I cannot wait for you to count the total number of swears in here. There are a lot.

1

They say it all started causa Cass but true I don't know Cass for shit. Well true I know her a little at least I think. I *mighta* talked to her last night at least I think. Also true what Cass says *mighta* happened. I dunno I can't say exactly causa I was kinda drunk. That's the only true thing I know for sure. Total that up that's alotta true against me and only one true for me and it's a pretty bad true. So the scales of justice are sorta tipped against me. It's true luck that Pup called to tell me what's going around about me before I go to school. I owe him one for sure causa otherwise I mighta walked right into the storm with no dealin plans whatsoever which mighta been true bad. Probably I'll hafta filch him that electric cattle prod he's always asking about from the hardware store. Probably that will end up bad for him. Or bad for me. Probably I'll lose my job. Anyway he said she said something happened with those funny guys from Memorial at the party and acourse now everyone is talking about it causa that's what always happens.

What were those funny guys from Memorial doing at the party anyway? *Who invited em?*

Causa it today I ditch school. I tell mom I'm sick which is only half true. Half lie. She calls me in so I don't hafta go to school and tells me take a hot bath and then she bolts to work. I go back to sleep instead. Now I gotta make up my mind about work. I'll ditch that too.

But I can't ditch forever or this thing is gonna spread like a wilderness fire til everybody says it and then it dogs me the resta my life til I leave town. I gotta go to work and deal. Holton will be there. Holton is always at the hardware store. *True Holton will be at the hardware store for the resta his life the dumb son a bitch.* He'll be there after school today and he'll be easy to turn. He's a football guy though not much a one. He's soft. He'll be easy to turn and that'll get the word right into the hornet's nest of it. It's a good place to start. True I'll go to work.

But first I gotta deal on Cass. What the hell happened with her anyway? *Did I bite her ear?* I can't remember exactly. The sink is full now and the drain is stopped and I dump the bowl of ice in. What happened? True it's a mess in my mind. But I'll tell all I know anyway.

I was talkin loud to Pup and Pete and Hokey drinking beer on the couch at the party.

Last night that much is true and clear in my memory.

Outta nowhere I felt sick and went to the bathroom. I tried to lock the door but I can't manage it. I stood in fronta the mirror and looked at myself and I was swaying and I knew I was into it. Water and lots of it. I opened the faucet and cupped my hands and held em under the spray and I drank til I was swelled up. My face and hair and shirt were all wet and I wanted to sleep bad. True water and sleep. I knew it true even then and I was too far in it really to know anything.

I sat down in the tub. I flung my legs over the edge and I rested my head. I closed my eyes. Then the door crept open and the guys from Memorial that I was talking about all came into the bathroom together laughing and talking. I opened my eyes for a second and they all stood over me looking at me. True their hair was combed perfect and their clothes were nice.

They said alotta stuff to each other but I didn't hear any of it really. I closed my eyes for a long time and fell asleep and then I opened em again. They took turns pissing and talking and then they were in fronta the mirror messing with their hair. I closed my eyes and slept again and they woke me up with a cold washcloth on my face. They patted my cheeks and even messed with my hair which was weird. But they gave me a big glass of cold water and I drank it straight down and I said thanks and they took the cup and I went back to sleep. True is that it? Think so. I opened my eyes and lifted my head. They were gone and the bathroom door was closed and I felt a lot better.

That's far as I remember clear at least. I look at myself in the mirror now. I take my shirt off and hold onto the sides of the sink. I dip my head into the ice water and the cold stings. Brainfreeze. I see Cass. *True I see Cass.* I remember her now.

She came into the bathroom right after the memorial guys left out I think. I opened my eyes and I was all sprawled out in

3

the tub. She looked at me with big eyes surprised and started creeping backwards all quiet. But I said it was OK and I started to get up but then I slipped and fell back into the tub and hit my head hard on the back edge. I groaned. She laughed but then asked if I was OK. I was fine and she said she had to pee. True she peed right there in fronta me. She must have been well into it too. I watched her pee for a second and she stared at me so I looked up at the ceiling.

I pull my head outta the ice water and grab a dry washcloth from the shelf and pat my sopping hair. I sink the washcloth into the ice water and wring it out. I rub my chest and armpits and put the cold cloth into my boxers and wash there too. True goosestuff. I remember some more.

She wiped and stood up and pulled up her pants while I looked up at some clouds of mildew. Then she talked to me. She talked to me though I can't remember about what or her actual words. But I remember the sound of her voice. True her voice was nice and kind and curious sounding.

She sat down in the tub next to me and we talked. We talked for a long time but I can't remember any of it. That's not true I remember asking if the door was locked and she said yes and then she kissed me. True she kissed me.

I lean out the bathroom door and throw the wet washcloth into the hamper and I look at the ice cold water and think I might dunk my head again. But I don't causa my head feels clean and clear now. True she kissed me.

That almost made up for the stuff they were saying. But still I hafta deal on that. True I hafta deal on it pronto. And it's gonna be a big dealin. That made me feel sick again. I dunk my head back into the water. This is a good way to get clean. Showers are for the wasters and the preeners. True preeners. Maybe I'll tell em all that. Every one of em assholes. But if I tell em that I won't be dealin and they won't ever stop saying what they're saying. That's how these things always go. I'll lay off it. I'll deal. Brainfreeze again til I pull up and gasp for air and dry my hair with a towel.

I Gotta go deal on Cass. That can't wait. I wonder what time it is? If she's home from school I'll go deal on her right now. But what if she has a job or plays sports or something? No she doesn't play sports. She was at the party wasn't she? Maybe she does. True I don't know the first thing about her except her voice is nice and she's kinda pretty and she kissed me. There is the peeing thing too but I can't say anything about that really. I can barely remember it.

2

I zip my hoodie zipper up and down up and down as I walk on the dirt shoulder of the State Road where it curves north toward town. Pup said on the phone he thinks Cass lives in a new development called *The Prentice* on the way into town. I'll walk through there on my way to work. What if there are a hundred houses? Simple. I'll look on the mailboxes for names. What's her last name? I don't even know. *True I'm dumb.* I'll walk through anyway. I got time and it's nice out. It's kinda hot out actually. I unzip my hoodie all the way down and pull it back over my shoulders.

I hear the faraway hum of an engine back around the bend of road. I look over my shoulder. Nothing yet just trees. True this is no deep South. It's not like they're gonna run me down in their truck or nail me to a tree or something. Hopefully true anyway. I got nerves all the same. True they might throw something at me out the window as they pass. I better run down this ditch and pop behind that big ole oakey tree there til they pass. Nope. Gotta deal. True dealin starts now.

The hum of the engine grows to a high whine. It's close now coming around the bend. It's not a truck I think. Too whiny. Look? Nope. Dealin. I push my fists into my pockets and pull my hoodie back up over my shoulders. I tighten up my fists. I tighten up everything.

Some old junky Buick with a tweaked fan belt screeches past. I hear the faint screeches of talk talk talk radio voices too. True a billion dollars I see that same Buick at the hardware store if I get there fast enough. Not true but a good bet anyway.

The trees over across the ditch stop off all of a sudden. They've been all chopped down on a clean line. Then there's *The Prentice*. Big houses and super big green yards with green crew cuts. *True the smell of fresh cut grass*. I cut across the shallow green ditch toward the entrance and I walk right past *The Prentice* sign. The ditch is super nice grass. It smells true good. I make sure to walk only on this side of a fake old rickety wooden fence so no one'll get pissed I'm walking here. It occurs to me they mighta used the chopped trees for the stupid fence and it mighta looked a whole lot realer but that would never happen. Not in a billion years.

The first mailbox says Preston. True first name for *The Prentice*. "Preston Prentice," I said out loud but quiet like so no one hears me and thinks I'm a nutter. *Preston Prentice*. The next mailbox seems a mile off and I'm hot as hell all of a sudden. I wipe my forehead and face with my sleeve. I'm soaked. I take off my hoodie.

It's hard to carry a hoodie in a normal way in your hands. I ball it all up but it's like I'm carrying a dead cat wrapped up or something. I tie it around my waist. Don't do that. It's stupid. Stop that. Don't be stupid. Just leave it there. It makes sense. It's hot and it has to go somewhere. True utility. *Mailbox Mitchell.* Another mile. *Mailbox Reed.* I check out the houses as I walk. Mongo. I get the feeling that no one has ever walked on this road. But there is kid stuff everywhere. Strollers. Dumptrucks. Trikes. They must go for walks. The houses are huge and they all look mostly the same set way back from the road behind football fields of perfect grass.

I pass a lady sweeping the walk near her front porch. She stops sweeping and stares at me. She stares at me for a long time with her mouth open a little bit. I wave to her. She stares at me for abouta billion years and then at last she closes her mouth and waves back. Her kid screams somewheres and she drops her broom and sorta half runs to the porch.

If they had left any big trees here I'd plop down in the shade on the perfect green grass and sleep for the rest of my life. True they cut all the trees down so strangers don't get attracted to nap on the lawns? Don't be stupid. True is true. There are no big trees here for a reason. Hell if I know what it is.

This ain't dealin I think. This is going for a pointless walk. I wonder if I can get outta the back of this place or if I'm gonna hafta double back. Maybe I'll be late for work if I hafta go back. Maybe I should go cut back now to get there on time. True not dealin.

First things first. How *exactly* am I dealin with Holton? Figure that out that's dealin. Start dealin. OK true Holton is soft. Why is he soft? He's big and kinda athletic and plays football but he doesn't start. Backup offensive lineman or something. Probably never plays. How the hell would I know that? Kinda pudgy. Kinda dumb. Kinda nice. Definitely not an asshole like the rest. He's a big hanger on. A lichen. A barnacle. *Moss*. They let em hang around causa he looks like em and laughs at their jokes. Even the jokes on him. He hangs on em causa he looks like em and doesn't know what the hell else to do. True he has no other interests. Football and the hardware store. That's it.

Oh man Holton is gonna be easy. True too easy. Mostly cruel. But it's gotta start somewheres. Dealins gotta be done. But what exactly then? *Think*. OK got it. I'll tell Holton there's a rumor going around about how he had sex with one of the fat donkeys they keep in the pen at the burrito place on 110. That's why the donkey was sick last spring. Donkey anal fissure. Vet tried to keep it quiet but Terry's mom volunteers there and she told Terry and Terry told Candice and so on. That's how these things always go. Everyone knows. Everyone's calling him Hee Haw Holton. True cruel. *Too cruel?*

Holton will forgive you. *Eventually*. He's too dumb not to. This is war and he's just the first hurt one. Holton will be the first casualty. Well besides me. More will get hurt. You can't hurt only the assholes. True assholes are too hard to hurt. So you gotta do proxies. You gotta work at angles and edges a little at a time til it's too much work for the real hardcore assholes to fight back. Then they move on. But innocents gotta get hurt. Stop with the dumb war thing. *It's not war.* It's just kid dealin that gots to get done. OK now I'm really dealin. *True dealin sucks.* That's enough til I get to the hardware store. Poor Holton don't know what's coming. *True Hee Haw Holton.*

Mailbox Edwards, Cook, Bailey, *Boring*, Brooks, Price, *Face-Punch Boring*, Hernandez. *Now there's something.* I didn't think I'd get a Hernandez here. But I guess even Hernandez is boring now too. I say it out loud, "Hernandez is boring." But not too loud causa that lady's probably back sweeping. Nice thing saying it. *True and good Hernandez is boring.*

3

I hear a faint tap tap somewheres in between the bird chirps and the low whir of a lawn mower and then there is a slick vinyl sounding sliding noise.

"Creepy stalker Joseph Kare!" Cass's nice voice yells out. True the voice more like echoes or maybe thunders across the great plains of lawn for everyone in every house in the Prentice and for the whole damn town to hear. True eraser of previous notes of kindness and of curiosity.

I see her angry face in a second story window. *Is it a hundred and fifty degrees out today?* Not legally true but sweat pours down my face anyway and I wish to god I didn't tie the hoodie around my waist. Instead I lift my arms and wipe my face on my shirt sleeve. I practically bury my whole face in my armpit to get the short sleeve across my forehead and mop up all the sweat. I stink. Soaked. True drenched. I'm OK with it. It's just me and I'm used to it. But gross to Cass for sure probably.

Then her angry face breaks up and she smiles wide enough for me to see her shiny teeth all the way across the green tundra. "We should talk," she says in a regular voice nice and quiet. Some kindness was back in her voice now but also some sadness or seriousness or something else like that. I open my mouth to answer but she slams the window down. I squint and nod at least just in case she's still looking at me from behind the glare.

The wood screen door cracks closed and she leaps down the steps three at a time and she comes at me across the lawn in a sprint. I kinda feel the urge to bolt. *How far to those trees?* But I stand there like that statue of Dave or Venus the Mild or something like that. True if I had no arms I couldn't wipe the sweat from my face. Cass might walk up and find me perfectly still and armless dripping in sweat like that picture of Richard Nixon Mr. Corvin showed us last year in debates. I wipe my face with both short sleeves and step onto the grass with a big awkward step like a Nazi marcher guy. Cass runs fast. True she must do sports.

I swing my arms casually as I walk casually across the soft green Antarctica toward her. But I hafta swing my arms kinda wide causa they keep running into my hoodie tied at my waste. That makes my walking about as casual as a old silverback Gorilla that's not used to walking upright. *True nervous and sweating perfuse too.* Her lawn is global. It takes forever for us to come together. It must take her dad all Saturday and parta Sunday to mow this thing. Whatever it takes he does a nice job of it though. Walking on it's like walking through a different really nice country. Maybe Monaco or some place like that.

Cass stops and I stop and she puts her hand on her hip and that pushes her other hip out the other way inside her jeans as a result. True goosestuff and sweat everywhere. "Hi Cass."

"Hello Joseph Kare!" She looks right into my eyes when she says it and she doesn't look away. I think hard for something to say but nothing comes. I look at the grass and I'm about to say something about how nice the grass is. *True enough about the goddamn grass.* "It's not nice what's going around about you Joseph," she hesitates but looks at me the whole time she talks without blinking even though the sun is blazing right on her face, "It's partly my fault Joseph you should know."

"Prime and true Cass," I say relieved she brought it up first, "Pup told me all about it and true it's part your fault. But it's all a mess."

"Why do you always say that Joseph?" The curiousness is back in her voice but it's mostly covered over by annoyance or something worse.

"Prime?" I thought about it some. "It's a sorta number. It's like the first number...but then it also means like a bunch more numbers after the first number...that's not the first number...alotta numbers actually. I never really understood it."

"No Joker, I meant *true*. Why're you always saying *true*?" She lets the stuff I said about the numbers pass.

"True true. I say it all the time." I nodded vigorously causing some sweat to drip off my chin.

"They should call you True not Joker." She smiles.

"I'd take either over what they're calling me now." When I say that her smile breaks away and she drops her head a little to one side.

"About that," she starts but stops again before going on, "it's not the worst thing they could be saying about you."

"That's true. But it's not true." It seems like a clear thing saying it.

"What's not true?" She looks puzzled.

"What they're saying ain't true." I clears things up.

"I know that Joseph. I was just saying that worse things can be said about a person. I'm talking about my part in this." She lifts her eyes as she speaks and makes a little nod the exact way Mrs. Shannon used to nod at me in third grade math when she asked me a question and waited for an answer. Back then if I didn't know the answer I just cried and Mrs. Shannon let me alone. I think about if that might work now and there is a long silence.

I open my mouth to say something but Cass goes on before I can. "I got caught in a conversation about it this morning at school Joseph."

She sure says my real name a lot. No one except my mom usually calls me it. "The girls asked me if something happened with you in the bathroom at the party and...and...and I said yes. I wasn't thinking. I just said it. I thought they were talking about me and you Joseph. Then I thought I was caught. I thought of all the awful things they were going to say about me. *You know what.*"

"True," I say unable to think of anything else to say and unsure exactly what I should know.

Cass gets an angry look on her face again. "But then Alex said that you and the guys from Memorial were in there together forever and I didn't say anything."

I nod and am about to say true but she cuts me off after just a little noise comes out. "I didn't say yes to Alex or anything Joseph. I said nothing. I was caught and I saw a way out and I said nothing. They took it from there. It took off after. Now everybody. I know it's wrong Joseph. I'll fix it. I'll talk to them about it and then they can talk about me instead."

"It's true," I say and Cass's face reddens. "They were in there with me for a long time. Those guys from memorial."

"I didn't know that Joseph." She sounds really surprised and then more than a little curious. "What happened?"

"Nothing. I mean I don't remember exactly what they said. I was kinda asleep for some of it. For most of it really. They peed and then they washed my face and gave me a glass of water," I told her straight and quick and then I blink a little trying to remember more.

"Joseph. They peed on your face?" she shouts at me and I look around to see if that lady was back at sweeping.

"No Cass. They peed in the toilet. Just like you," I explain to her quietly.

"Then why on earth did they wash your face?" She sounded puzzled. She looked puzzled.

15

"I think they were just being nice. I was pretty passed out." I think about it again and it *was* nice of em. I decided that I probably owed em for it. I wondered if there was anything at the hardware store that I can filch for em. Probably not.

"That *is* nice Joseph," she says.

"It was true nice. It sobered me up a lot," I said it and then I go quiet for a few seconds. "True nice with you after too Cass."

She looks at me a long time unblinking like she was looking for something particular before she answered, "Still, it's really not fair what they are saying about you. I'll make it right."

"No Cass. I'm dealin. I have a plan." I start to think about who next after Holton. After Holton it hasta be a true hardcore asshole. Someone who deserves it and not another innocent. *True protocol for dealin.*

"Let me guess," she smiles, "a true plan?"

"Tried and true." I make a Chesire Cat sorta smile back at her.

"Will you tell me?" she asks.

But before I can answer her dad, who was already standing on the lawn by the porch, shouts to us, "Cassandra, is your new friend going to stay for dinner?"

I wonder how long he'd been standing there and if maybe he heard Cass shouting about the Memorial guys peeing on my face. Cass turns and looks at me and I shout back to her dad, "Thanks sir but no. I hafta be to work in a few."

"Ah...a working man." Her dad shakes his head up and down all happy and smiles at me.

"Not legally true on either count I think sir," I shout but sorta quiet back across the green fairway at her father. "Only fifteen sir...I got a few years til actual manhood. And the hardware store doesn't pay enough to be categorized legally as a job. It's more like volunteering or an internship. You ever volunteer at an old folks home sir? It's kinda like that."

Cass sniggers and covers her mouth with her hand. Cass's Dad looks at me with his mouth open and his head all cocked sideways. They must not have any flies at the Prentice causa they're mouths are sure open a lot here. I'm pretty sure he missed what I said but he didn't say what or anything.

"I'm going in for dinner. Good luck with the plan." Cass stares at me without blinking again for probably acoupla hours. "Remember Joseph, even good plans go bad. Will you tell me all about it tomorrow?" She walks backwards from me slowly waiting for an answer.

"True tomorrow I'll have stuff to tell." She shakes her head as I answer and then she turns and runs. Runs fast. *True lightness and sweetness everywhere as she sails away from me across the green sea.* Must be sports. I'll hafta ask. I'll also hafta ask how old she is. I'll hafta ask everything really.

4

OK I hafta do acoupla quick things now. I'll do it super fast I promise causa it's gonna be kinda boring. *True boring.* But Mrs. H. says I hafta causa it's the legal way to do this sorta thing. We fought about it actually. We had alotta fights actually. I've won only one or two of the fights as you will see in a sec. But true I don't mind fighting Mrs. H. It's fun really but that's a secret. Not a true secret obviously.

Here's a trick I just thought of so you can skip over the boring part. I'll put "Duck Duck Goose" in here just like that when the boring part is over and the story part is actually back going. That way you can just skip ahead and start reading where it says that. OK go if you wanna.

OK there's two things about this you should probably know. I'm not supposed to swear in here. Like at all. But I'm gonna swear anyway. As you know I started right out with a swear in here and that was the biggest fight of all with Mrs. H. I knew what I was doing really and I won that fight believe it or not. But

I promised to keep it to a very low number of total swears.

Then I lost acoupla fights on purpose after just to make it even again. But I really have a plan about the swears. My idea is that once the story really gets going it doesn't matter what the actual words are causa you just pass right over em rushing to get to the next one. So I plan to sneak in more and more swears as we go. By the end it will be full of em and you won't even notice. My whole point about this is that I like swears and I want em in here. There are tons of swears in real life anyway and it's my story. And I want it like that. That's it really.

I guess you can say I was dealin on Mrs. H to get more swears in here. I guess you can say I'm always dealin. But I'm not. *True I'm not I swear.*

The only other thing I'm supposed to put in here is about me. Mrs. H. only *kinda* won this fight and I'm gonna *kinda* do it. But I'm gonna do it like I want. Not like she wants. She says you need to know more about me. About my background. About my mom. About my house which is kinda old. About what I wear when I sleep and what I dream about when I sleep and what I eat for breakfast and important things in my basement and that sorta thing and on and on and everything. *Blah blah!* I think you already know enough. Way too much. So I'll just say it like this: I'm not smart, OK? I'm not retarded or legally disabled or anything like that acourse. I've actually been tested about it and let's just say I'm not smart.

OK there is one small not true thing in that last part and that is that I actually tested better acoupla times recently and that's really the last thing I hafta tell you I swear. That and I read alotta books. Alotta books. That's partly causa Mrs. H. and partly causa my mom. But mostly I just like it. I buy em all the time and get em sent to my house in the mail boxes. That's the only reason I have a stupid hardware store job. Books. That's it. Bingo. But it's not like I read the bible or anything. It's just stuff I like to read about space mostly and adventures and that sorta thing but also true ones.

I even bought a book last month about fixing my mom's crappy ole Ford Taurus. I made a plan to fix her AC before summer came on and I turned sixteen. I suck at math but even I can add up that dates plus sweating plus my mom's crappy ole Ford Taurus with no AC equals a shit summer. See I have a big plan for dates this summer and it looks already like my plan is going good. I fixed the AC on the crappy ole Ford Taurus and now there is this sorta thing with Cass as you already know. Anyway I ended up reading the whole damn Taurus book anyway. Oh my god this is so boring. Mrs. H. I hope you are happy now. OK Duck Duck Goose.

I get my vest on at the hardware store and put my hoodie in the little locker in the back room and I drink a bunch of water causa I sweated out all of the water in my body walking through the goddam Prentice. The vest is nice and light. It is actually pretty cool in the store despite the fact that the AC has been broken for fifty years at the very least.

There's a little neon orange patch on the vest and I'll give you only one guess what it says. It says "Bolton's Hardware." That's right if you can believe it. This is Holton's dad's store and Holton's full name is actually Holton Bolton if you can believe that. Holton's dad and mom actually gave him that as a name. I mean giving a guy that name is like a legally binding contract for him to be a true moron.

Speaking of Holton when I come out onto the floor he's next to the pallet of topsoil bags and he looks right at me with a big smile like the Chesire Cat and a big bright pink face like a pig and big white moon eyes. I stop and look at him and I think he might explode. True dealin starts right now. But then the dinger goes off and some kid bolts through the front door and slips sideways into the fasteners isle. OK Holton you get a stay of execution.

I find the kid staring down at the nail bins. He's about my age. No he's probably acoupla years older. Maybe eighteen but he's real skinny or maybe wiry is a better way to say it so it's hard to tell. His hair is all slicked and he's wearing a nerd white button up shirt tucked into black slacks that are jacked up about to his neck. *True nerd.* Nervous too. He looks like he's gonna explode or something. True exploding idiots everywhere in the hardware store. He stands there and looks at me for like ten minutes with his mouth open like he sees a true ghost. True I better start getting used to open mouths around

21

me. I wave my hand between us and he snaps outta it.

"Need help with em nails?" I ask.

"Uh. Yeah." He stares down at all the nails and doesn't look at me when he talks. "I need five pounds."

"Which ones?" I ask.

"Uh..." He looks at the nails for a long time.

"What are you building?" I ask

"Something with my dad." He hesitates for another sec and then points his arms out spasmodically at the framing nails and then sorta yelps at me, "These!"

"OK OK," I calm him down. I grab a box and I fill it and weigh it all the time looking at him with him all the time looking at the nails and then I take the box up to the counter.

All the time I'm ringing up the explosive nerd Holton stands right next to me staring at me like six inches from my face. He crosses his arms and rocks back and forth on his heels and he grins and shines almost bright red like Rudolph. It's xmas AM for Holton I swear. Then the dinger goes off again when the nail nerd vacates the place and Holton practically bends over and shouts into my face.

"Devin says that you and those guys from Memorial at the party in the bathroom..." He sprays bits of spittle onto my face as he shouts and I think about how I can really use those guys from Memorial with their washcloth right now.

Then I place my hand gently on Holton's

shoulder and hold it there and then I start to pat his shoulder nice and gentle and slow a few times. He stops talking and looks at my hand with his mouth open. *True a whole world full of mouth breathers.*

"I know I know Holton. It's not true. None of it. True false. It's all just a big game your buddies are playing Holton. Let em play. I wouldn't worry about it." I speak slowly practically whispering and then I pause and we both look at my hand on his shoulder for a sec before I start up again much louder this time. "Actually there is some small cause for worry. Something *you* might wanna worry about. I heard about it today."

His eyes sorta pop outta his head and he leans in to listen as he waits for me to finish. He's too excited. He wants to say everything so badly. *Everything.* But before he can say any of it I start talking and his bulging eyes start to shrink back into his big pig or cow skull and I can almost see the things I say slowly soak into his tiny little brain through his eyes.

Then I hit him with the donkey thing and he shrivels all up right in fronta me like a leaky balloon. *True shrink.* I actually feel really bad for him and I pat him on the shoulder some more. Now it's real dealin. I tell him everything the way I said it to you but I add in little things that come into my mind as I go. I say that his neighbor Ben noticed Holton leaving his house very late on the night in question. I say that the Anderson kid that lives just across 110 from the burrito place remembered being woken up by terrible animal screams on that very night. And lastly I tell him and I swear I had no intention of saying it but I tell him that Mr. Stafford at The Sentinel has the whole thing researched and written up and that he was only waiting for the story to clear legal before it goes to print.

The part about the paper was too far I think. It must be something about the hard facts of actual printed words on paper that does it. Holton starts crying right there in his own hardware store. First his eyes suck way back into his head some more like they are cowering or something trying to hide from a nasty beast predator which is me acourse. Then the holes where his rabbit eyes are hiding fill up with a ocean of water that pours down his pink face. True oh shit. I can't help myself. These things always happen. *True too far.*

I pat his shoulder wildly now. I smack the guy as hard as I can trying to get him calmed down but he's crazy like one of those tragedy ladies all blubbering and wailing. Jesus this is bad. Then I hug him. I actually hug him if you can believe it. I hug big ole pig head Holton Bolton right in my arms in the middle of his own hardware store and that finally does it. *True I'm a monster.* I mean I actually make up crap and lay it on a guy bad enough that I hafta hug him so he doesn't actually shit his pants or die from crying or something like that.

Holton calms down and I go back to patting him gentle. I start to worry that this thing I made up was too much and that he might never talk about it again which will completely ruin the dealin plan. So I try to turn it back around.

"Don't worry Holton. I'll talk to my mom. She kinda knows the vet. I mean they had to work together on his building permit and everything. I bet she can convince him to destroy everything and everything." He nods dumbly as I talk. "But someone's gotta talk to the guys. I mean you don't want to get kicked off the team. I'd talk to em myself but I'm kinda in everybody's dog house right now as you know."

"But Joker it's a lie," Holton pleads his case to me.

"I know I know Holton. At least that's what we've got to convince the guys at any rate." I look at him with some hope.

"I'll do it Joker. The guys like me OK. They'll have lotsa laughs on it." He frowns and ponders the inevitable for a moment. "It's gonna be bad for a while..."

"It's gonna be bad for you and me both Holton." I smack his shoulder one last time as hard as I possibly can but he doesn't even notice. He just stares outta his little cave hole into some future thinking about some far worse pain than the little sting on his shoulder. "But we'll make it through. Together."

I really want Holton to stop staring off into space in that painful way so I try to change the subject on him. "You know who that nail nerd was that just left?"

That sorta snaps him outta it. "Um, yeah, that's Edward Something. He lives on the Schmidt farm way out on the River Road."

"Huh," I say trying to pretend I'm interested which I wasn't.

"His family rents the small house on the far side." He pauses and the pained look creeps back onto his face. "They call him Ed the Goat."

"Who calls him Ed the Goat? I didn't even know he went to school?" I see where this is going now and I see why the pain is back on his face and I know I screwed it up trying to get it off his face this way.

"No he doesn't go to school. He's homeschooled. But the kids on the bus. You know when they pick up the Schmidt kids. They seen him petting the Goats and they named him Ed the Goat." Great. Holton's face was all screwed up again with tragedy now and he staring off.

"Goats?" I say sorta forgetting my plan of getting the pain off his face. "I thought the Schmidt place was a sod farm."

"It is." Holton kinda comes back to reality again. "But they have a apple orchard in the front part of the farm where you can pick apples in the fall. They got a few Goats there. You know. For the kids to pet and feed and stuff when you're picking apples."

Holton looks much better now that he's talking about stuff so I just hafta keep him going. But then I blurt out this thing that I have no idea whatsoever I'm gonna do and then it's just completely ruined. "Ed the Goat and Hee Haw Holton. You guys should be friends."

True Jesus Christ I'm a terrible person. True Duck Duck Goose.

5

I think about Cass for the resta my shift and then more on the walk home which was cooler thankfully causa the sun was down. That mostly works and helps things some about what I did to Holton but not enough really. Even in high school it's a delicate balance on the scales of justice when you total up good and evil for yourself and other peoples. Now my scale is way tipped over to the bad side. *True bad.* To be honest I don't really buy good and evil at all. That's strict church people blubbering. But whatever it is really it's not good for me right now with Holton on my own scale of it so I hafta set up my next parta dealin to fix it somewhat if possible.

On the walk home in the coolness it is much easier to think clear about it and get it set up. Still acoupla trucks pass with their high lights shooting down at me and that jumbles me up and almost sends me into the trees again. But I keep right on walking and get it figured out. Here's one thing I learned though. At least hold your breath after trucks pass by you for a sec. They kick alotta stuff up and it swirls behind em and that will keep the dirt and dust outta your mouth.

So here it is true straight the plan. I will sit tight just one day or part of it. That's all it will take for Holton to blubber to his fake buddies if he hasn't blubbered already. Then I'll just listen real good around school if I can. I'll ask if I hafta. And whoever is spreading it worst about Holton that dude is going to get the next. That is the next hurt and next dealin part of the plan. Wait a minute come to think of it the next worst person is gonna probably be a girl. It's always a girl. They are the worst about this stuff. So I hafta think about that. But whatever at least I have a dealin plan in place.

This gets me real pumped on for the rest of the walk and I'm ridin high. But then I feel bad again causa what I did to Holton so I need to come up with something else to make it OK. I search around in my brain and remember that part in that super old movie Rambo when Rambo yells, "That king shit cop drew first blood!" That gets me real pumped up. I actually walk off the side of the road and cut through the trees some and I imagine I am true Rambo for like five whole minutes before I feel stupid and go back to the road. *Not true Rambo*. Rambo is a badass and that's a cool movie but this is true and not at all like the movies. The only true way to do it is to tell Holton and say sorry. Simple as that. I'll do it soon. But not just yet acourse I'm not perfect.

I sleep bad that night as you can imagine but there

is some good parts thinking about Cass again. Some real good parts if you catch my drift. *True nothing like it in the very beginning like it is now with Cass.* Just somehow I hope the feeling can last for a little while longer though I don't see how with this tempest blustering up in our town or at least in our high school. That was for you Mrs. H. Everyone else can skip it. Duck Duck Goose.

True the next day at school is the worst day of my life as you can expect. Well legally false as I am only sixteen so for sure there is gonna be worse days from now. Oh now is also a good time to tell you that what I said to Cass's dad about being fifteen was also legally false. I just turned sixteen but I still forget and say fifteen. This is a real big problem for me that you oughta know. I say things over and over and actually practice em til they just come out and it takes a long time for me to get em outta my brain or fix em when they become legally false. So stuff like that thing about being fifteen and not a man I actually literally practiced that til it became kinda like a habit. It's gonna take acoupla months til I can switch it around to be sixteen not fifteen.

I'm not weird or anything I'm not like a Tom Cruise actor who sits in front of the mirror and practices all night long talking to skulls. But my mind does go a lot and it does sorta say things over and over. This is actually a secret thing that I want to tell if you are still a kid or maybe even a adult. It will probably help you a lot. I don't know anything. Well false acourse but what I mean is that I don't know alotta stuff and I'm not smart like I said already but usually I have something to say at least that sounds OK.

This is partly causa the reading but it's mostly just causa I practice saying things in my brain. I don't try to do it or even think about it. It just sorta happens. That's mostly how these things just come outta my mouth all the time. Here's the deal I don't know jack shitola about anything and neither do you but I can usually at least say two sentences about whatever I have to that don't make me sound like a complete retard caveman idiot. I swear nearly every damn thing people say in class sounds like a retarded dog is barking.

So that's my whole secret and it applies to the whole world in fact and not just high school. Nobody knows anything but a few people can say something that's not true dumb and these people get to do pretty much whatever the hell they want OK? Some not true things about this that I just thought about. I mean the moon obviously and satellites and those sorts of big and hard things. I mean when a professor or a NASA Nerd shoots a satellite to the moon and it actually doesn't blow up then they are actually not morons like you and me. Holy super boring. Duck Duck Goose.

You ever walk into a burning building? I mean not to save a kid or something like a hero I mean like actually just walk into a building say to buy a Coke or a bag of chips and then realize that the whole damn place is on fire? Like really super hot and burning with flames and falling down around you? That's what it feels like when I walk into school today. I mean everyone shoots flames of fire right at me even the goddamn secretary Mrs. Pierce looks at me like I have a scorpion for a head and she wants very bad to smash me with a giant hammer or I mean burn me to death with her flames of fire eyes (is that better Mrs. H.?).

But what are you gonna do when you're dealin but keep on dealin? So I deal on. I go to my locker acourse nice and slow and cool. Especially cool in fact on account of all the flames of fire eyes. Now this AM locker visit normally takes two seconds and I'm off but today I linger there for like five minutes. This is real dealin this morning causa some of Holton's blood brother footballers are giving it to me good at my locker. But I just smile at em and mention something about how they wear a mask that they're growing into only I say it better than that. Thanks for that one Mrs. H. by the way it really works.

This is a key thing to dealin you know. Dealin isn't all that hard really if they aren't already punching you in the face or likely to punch you in the face. I place my bets at my locker that Holton's buds are not in a true punching mood. I say this thing and it's enough to shut em up for a second while they figure it out. See it's vital for em to figure it out if I'm saying something bad about em or not. It's like life or death for em to figure it out before everyone else figures it out and it's too late for em. That's the key. That's when you either get a nice pause to walk away or you get punched in the face. I get away this morning.

But I do go away nice and slow and I hear Jamie the mostly main leader guy saying something about my Holton donkey story. This always happens or at least a lot anyway. If you screw em up even the tiniest little bit they will turn on someone else. It's fear or at least the tiniest seed of fear in the dark moldy little mushroom garden of their minds. That's my whole dealin plan in a nutshell really as you know. But now I know I hafta deal direct with Jamie causa that was the phase two part of the plan.

Acourse it's straight to the top with Jamie causa he's like the main captain of the circus clowns or whatever. I really secretly hoped it was gonna be some bitchy girl but it is what it is. Remember it's still the scales of justice in high school thing for me causa what I did to Holton too so it's no other direction but straight to the top dealin.

I go nice and slow and cool all the way to gym. I'm like Sherlock Interpol listening to everything I hear along the way. True I don't hear one thing about my problems or Holton's problems but still I listen. Sure I get alotta flames of fire eyes but nothing too bad really. What I shoulda done was start thinking on the Jamie dealin but still I hafta stick to my big plan and do the general listening first.

Let me tell you about gym for a sec. I go to gym first period. I like gym OK. I like all my classes OK which I'm sure makes me the weirdest person in the history of the world. But really I only find it boring when the teacher is boring which is really alotta the time as you know if you've ever had a teacher. But even when that happens I kinda find other ways to not get bored like doing things in class like activities or reading about things the teacher is supposed to be teaching us which you already know I do anyway.

Anyway the one bad thing about gym first period is that I sweat a lot. Like really a lot as you already saw with what I did in a pool of my own sweat in Cass's yard area. This means acourse I absolutely hafta shower after every first period so I don't smell like a cow or a horse or something the rest of the day. Trust me I am no male model or anything but this does go back to my plan about summer that I told you about. There is a part of getting summer dates where you must not smell like a horse or a cow. That's one of those life lessons if you didn't know it.

Hold on a sec. I need to start a new chapter causa this next part is kinda long and also pretty bad. *True bad really.*

6

OK I just thought of another thing I gotta do. You know how I said this part is kinda bad? Well it really is. It's probably bad enough really that I gotta do another little trick about it. Remember the Duck Duck Goose trick for boring parts? Well if you're a young kid or something or some kinda sensitive person that pukes at the sight of blood this part might be bad enough that you should skip over it. It's gonna make it kinda hard to follow after but it's better to skip ahead than just quit. I'll try to keep it simple so you can follow it after and just know that something bad happened. Anyway here's how I'll do this one. I'll just put "Grand Central Station" in here when the really bad part is over so just skip ahead for that.

I guess if you're a really young kid you don't even know what a Grand Central Station is. But this is not a dictionary of that kinda thing so just trust me it has to do with trains and things going every which way.

So our gym class is kinda crazy. It has if you can believe it a huge purple satellite painted on the wall.

You know for sure that you are in a new kinda school when it's called after a satellite. That's what we are. The Satellites. Most schools get stuff like Tigers or Spartans or named after birds or something but nope we got Satellites. As you can imagine this drives most kids here crazy and they think it's the dumbest name and they're embarrassed to say they're from it. But as you know I'm actually kinda into space and I actually kinda like it. Sorry that has nothing to do with the story really but at least you know what the gym looks like and one thing about our school.

We did track indoors that morning. It's important. *True important.* We run around in a circle and relay off those sticks to each other and I'm not the fastest runner in the world but I'm OK and I'm the second to last leg and our last guy is a really fast skinny runner and we win. We actually beat a team that is all Holton's buddies including Jamie and this one other guy that I hafta tell you about. He's Jeff and this is where it starts to get bad. Things always start to get bad around this guy Jeff trust me.

As you can imagine causa all the stuff going on already about me that me being part of the winning team over these football guys is a big thing. Especially for Jeff. Let me just tell you acoupla things about Jeff so you get the idea. You know I said Jamie was like the circus master or whatever. Well Jamie can be pretty bad but really he's not that bad and I mostly have him figured out. I mean it's easy to see he wants people to like him and he wants to look tough but under all that he's OK really. I know it's hard to believe I'm saying it.

35

But this Jeff guy is another kinda thing. You know how there is always this one kid in your school who like kills small animals or something? That's Jeff. Only he doesn't just kill small things like some stupid cat or birds or something with a BB gun. I mean if you read in the news abouta dog dying or even a cougar or mountain lion dying mysteriously or something then immediately everybody thinks of Jeff. I mean nobody says it out loud causa they're really afraid Jeff will actually kill em if he hears it. *True kill em*. Jeff is that kinda guy. True pure mean and cruel and dangerous.

All that stuff I said before about the plan and dealin with these guys and how you can say stuff and not get punched in the face sometimes? Well don't ever even do any dealin stuff with Jeff types. That type punches you acourse but then they also jump outta some dark alleys some night later like a maniac and really hit you right on the head with a tire iron or a rusted naily board or something. Really bad acourse.

So after the race thing Jeff the angry baboon's face turns as bright red as a baboon's red ass when we beat em in the race. The other guys on my team are smart apparently causa they all disappeared god knows where. But I'm true dumb acourse causa I'm standing there by myself and Jeff comes over and shoves me right over onto the ground. I slide like partway across the gym and get acoupla nice good burns on my leg and shoulder. I start to say something bad to him but then I remember the rule about the dead cougars and mountain lions and I hold onto my tongue. But still I stand up and tell Jeff sorta polite that he might wanna lose a little more graceful in races.

This is still bad for Jeff to hear acourse and he comes at me again but this time Jamie and the other circus baboons hold him back the way circus baboon's always do that. And thankfully Mr. Huggies the gym teacher shows up right then and says the dumbest things that teachers always say in these situations like "Now Now Fellas." As if that sorta thing ever did anything ever in the whole history of fights in gym class. At least Mr Huggies being there made Jeff stop off a killing me for a few minutes.

His name is not really Mr. Huggies acourse. Everyone just calls him that causa he always says this stupid thing to get us going in gym class. He says, "Hugga Lugga Loo kids!" It never gets us going but he says it all the time anyway and everyone is used to it. He's a military guy like a former general or something and he has a really gray old crew cut. He's in shape kinda on the top a his body but his bottom half is kinda dumpy and he wears these blue gym shorts that are too tight and it does actually kinda look like he's wearing a diaper under em. So that is also where Mr. Huggies comes from.

Off to the showers. Makes me sick a little even to think about it now but oh well. I'm showering away as part of my plan for summer dates. I'm kinda off to one corner in the showers and some of the circus baboons are hooting and hollering and beating on their chests in the far corner of the showers. Everyone else acourse is smart again and completely not there. I mighta known right then it was a true bad situation.

I push the button on the soap thing on the wall and catch the soap in my hand and start washing my armpits and I turn a bit as I do this just in time to see Jeff's fist coming at the side of my head. It's bad. I fly right against the wall and I acourse ended up with a big black eye later. Not from where Jeff hit me in the side of my head but where my other eye smashed up against the wall.

Jeff hits me one more time but I actually get off a good kick into his nuts and he falls backwards. But then every other one of the other circus baboons is on me but strangely they are not pummeling me as I was expecting. Instead they are holding me down. I acourse kick and scream and actually get some good hits in.

Now I'm not a professional wrestler or anything as you can imagine. I just realized that you have no idea what I actually look like. Well it's too late now really. I don't wanna just tell you now and ruin it for you whatever you got setup for me to look like in your brain. Let's just say I look pretty regular sized but I have some muscles that you can't really see. Thank god for it too causa what was happening to me in the shower. It really helped some. I get enough good hits in that Jeff pushes the guys off that was holding me down. I think it was Eric he pushed mostly but I don't remember. So now Jeff's holding my arms and this baboon is strong enough that I can't get any good hits in anymore.

Then Jeff turns me over so my face is facing down and then Jeff yells for Jamie to come on. Jamie comes on behind me and I see he has the stick from the track running. The baton or whatever and I don't mean the thing that some girls throw up and twirl around you know. Then Jeff yells at him to fuck me with it. I know that's probably too bad a swear to use in here but it's a bad situation and way worse words are actually used so I hafta put in at least one of the really bad words. Then Jeff says alotta other stuff I'm sure you can imagine causa the thing going around about the Memorial guys and how I will like it. It's all bad stuff. You can just imagine it OK.

So then Jeff really yells at Jamie to do the thing. I see Jamie upside down through my legs. I see clear and true that he is scared outta his mind. Then this other funny thing happens. I swear I see Mr. Huggies just outside of the shower for a sec then too. I mean just for a sec and then he's gone. I mean maybe he saw it and left but I can't say for sure.

Then Jamie hits me on the back with the stick and it wasn't even that hard. This drives Jeff absolutely crazy. He's so mad at Jamie that I think for a sec he's actually gonna drop me and instead kill Jamie. But acourse he doesn't. Then I feel it. I feel the stick pushing up at my thighs and cutting some on my skin and stinging real bad acourse you know where and I panic real bad and kick wild like and scramble in my mind for ideas.

Then I think Jeff relaxes a little bit causa he was so happy that Jamie was actually finally doing it.

That's when I pull my head up real hard and hit Jeff in the chin. This stuns him a sec and he screams pretty bad but he doesn't let go and right then I bite him right on the cheek. I don't mean like a small bite or a nibble or something. I mean I bite him full hard really serious. I even bite some of his cheek right off so it's serious. This is one thing I never said sorry about ever even though I ended up getting suspended about it. This was a bad situation and I did this thing that was bad but I have thought about it like a billion times and I would do it again and again.

So whether it's causa I bit Jeff in the face or causa Mr. Huggies is now in the shower breaking it up it's all over then. There is blood everywhere swimming around the drains. Jeff is bouncing off the walls crazy and screaming and holding his cheek which is bleeding completely everywhere. I just sit there like some kinda naked cougar with Jeff's blood all over my face and some blood running down off my thighs. That stupid stick was thank god floating away on the floor and not stuck forty feet into in my ass. Jamie just sits there shaking against the wall. *He's true scared.* I have not heard him say one word since that day at all so it was not just a temporary scared thing either.

Grand Central Station.

7

Jeff got expelled acourse. This is probably the one thing about this whole situation that will not make you think the world is turned all around and broken. I don't even think he woulda got expelled if he was not such an angry baboon. He couldn't even lie about the whole thing. He just said right out what he wanted to do and why he wanted to do it and that I deserved it and they expelled him causa it. The other baboons had enough brains at least to lie about it and say it was just a fight. They just got suspended like me.

Now why I got suspended I never understood exactly. I guess it's causa I bit part of Jeff's face off and that made me like a Hannibal Lecture Hall or something and there is a legal rule about having to suspend Hannibals. The way I see it is the world is at least somewhat turned around and broken when a guy gets almost stick ass raped at school and he gets suspended. I mean for a high school level this is kinda as bad a thing as some of the really bad stuff happens in Africa. True injustice everywhere

41

in the world at the high school levels and Africa levels.

So you see that Mr. Huggies did come back in after all. I don't know but I think he was there and then left and then came back. Whether it was causa he wanted to let it happen for a little bit before for he came back in or whether he left and then changed his mind I'll never know. Maybe I just imagined it which is possible. But funny thing is the stick baton did disappear somewhere and they never found it at all. That's how these things always go. Maybe that is why Jeff was not legally arrested and put in jail which is what shoulda happened anyway. I mean the cops were there and everything and they did their Sherlock Interpol thing but nobody was ever thrown legally in jail.

Believe it or not two good things actually happen about this. One is that all the talk about me mostly goes away. I mean what's the use of talking crap abouta kid who just got attempted stick ass raped or murdered on? Even all the retarded dog barking kids can see that clear enough. So I am mostly done on this part of it. Though not really true as you will see. But my dealin is mostly done for sure. I don't really hafta do much else for the plans. I have to work for Holton some here and there though to get that one to go away. Oh and I do actually eventually tell Holton Bolton the donkey part is all my fault and I do say sorry. He is really angry and doesn't talk to me for a while but I have a smashed up face pretty bad so I think that helps and he forgives me.

The other good part is about Cass. The next night after the big thing in the shower she invites me over for dinner. My mom lets me have the crappy ole Ford Taurus to drive over there which was really good. I don't drive straight there but do a big loop first out by the River Road. I see the Schmidt farm but there are no goats anywhere that I can see. I wonder for a minute if Holton was making things up about the Goat Ed kid and the goats but then finally I see a little pen off the big barn kinda close to the apple trees so I figure they must be in the barn. But really who am I kiddin? Holton Bolton would never in a billion years make something up on his own.

I actually park just up the road a ways from the Schmidt farm causa my side trip is not gonna take me near long enough to get me there on time. There is a really nice little dirt pull out type area in a batch of trees on the higher side of the road. The Schmidt farm sits way low down off the river road and it stretches for what seems like a hundred miles out to the actual river the road is talking about. And like Cass's yard the whole farm is true green all the way out to the river causa like I said it's a sod farm. So I just sit there looking at it for a long time causa as you probably guessed it already I like grass a lot. But don't worry I'm not gonna go on about it.

The main house of the Schmidts is huge but really old and it sits right in the middle of the farm close to the River Road. The little orchard Holton talked about is also near the road close to where I'm parked. There is a big barn right behind the orchard where the goat pen I was talking about is. There is also a little tiny old house just a shack really on the far side of the Schmidt house sitting way back off the road. That must be where Goat Ed is I think. There is a dirt driveway that runs all the way back to it and there is a rotten old dirty white van parked out front. A light is on in the window and I watch it for somebody in there but I see nobody.

I see a bunch of little tank trucks driving super slow as you can imagine back and forth back and forth across a bunch of little dirt roads cut into the continent of green grass. I watch em for a long time killing my time for Cass's. They spray some yellow stuff all onto the sod grass. As I did the watching just then a little goat comes outta the big barn into the pen so I got legal Sherlock Interpol evidence that Holton Bolton is not a legal liar after all. Duck Duck Goose now it's time to get going to Cass's.

Wait I forgot one more thing too on the Schmidts. Right as I'm driving off I catch outta the corner of my eye Goat Ed comes running outta the house and around to the back of it. And then this real old guy comes out too musta been his dad or granddad and he waves his hand around in the air like a maniac and he shouts god knows what after Ed. I can't hear it acourse causa the AC is cranked but it sure looks like Goat Ed has it true bad in alotta ways. *True no surprise Goat Ed's always got it bad at home.* OK true Duck Duck Goose to Cass's now.

The real reason for my big loop in the old crappy Ford was not to do some Sherlock Interpoling on

Holton's story. It was to blast the goddamn air conditioner for a long time before going to Cass's. It's getting close to summer now and it's hot as hell out even in the late part of daytime. I had a kinda nice shirt on too. Not tucked in or anything I mean I'm not a ass kisser or anything but it's kinda a nice shirt. I was kinda starting to sweat right through it just causa walking to the car so I really had to go for this long drive with the AC cranked up so I can get over to Cass's not looking like a creature that just jumped up outta like a wet swamp.

Luckily I left like a whole hour early before dinner was really supposed to start. To be honest this is not part of my plan but just happened and the reason it happened was causa I was nervous as hell OK. *True nervous.* I mean I know you know that I read alotta books and that I've had some experiences in life like the AC thing and that I do dealin and do plans and stuff like that. But I really don't have any real experiences with girls except for some minor leagues bases stuff if you know what I mean. So this is a big deal thing for me and I don't mean dealin like I talked about before. There is one more part of this about why I am so nervous that I also hafta put in here. I think I am part in love with Cass already OK. *There.*

So it's one thing to just be with Cass alone knowing this part of how I feel about her. But it's way worse to hafta be with her and her parents too at the same time causa it. Good feelings and bad feelings and nerves go all really mixed together if you know what I mean. If not here is one thing that happens that will show it better.

When I do get there Cass comes to the door right before I knock and she's wearing this small type shirt that is real thin on her shoulders and really there is not much fabric in the shirt at all. I mean it's hot out so it makes sense and everything but just so you know Cass has some real nice breasts and they're also kinda big. I'm not sure if that's the legally best way to say that about her. I mean you never hear other people talking about stuff like that in a way that is legally true. Unless acourse you are reading a Shake Spear Love Poem or something. Anyway I mean what I say about her breasts in as nice a possible way. I mean when I see her behind the screen at the door and that shirt on her breasts makes me feel in a certain way. I'm not sure how to make you get it exactly except maybe to say I feel really hot again but also very lighted up and happy to be alive and right there at the door.

So she opens the door and she gives me this big long hug which makes everything I was feeling way worse than it already is which is impossible believe me. She then feels around my skin on my face and around my big black eye and she says nice things about this stuff. I feel her warm breath right on my face as she talks and this feeling just gets worse and worse or more and more or probably better and better or however you might say it. It's just really strong that's all. I know I know I'll stop talking about it now.

Then both of her parents are standing right there behind her all of a sudden and they say hello to me and it's a big mixup of feelings. That's what I was talking to you about the mixup of feelings. I feel bad about feeling this stuff with her parents standing there but I also kinda hate em and just want em to go away. I want to actually take Cass away from em a little bit. I don't really hate em acourse and I'm not gonna kidnap her but I just kinda feel it.

OK now I'm just messing it up more so let's just go to the dinner part. Instead let's just go to the after dinner part causa dinner was fine and real good food and everything and I talked to her parents real nice. But let's just go to the after dinner part. Duck Duck Goose.

8

OK I made a whole new chapter for this part even though the last chapter was hardly even a chapter at all. The thing is that this part coming on really deserves to be kinda set off aside all alone in it's own part. I mean it really true has to be that way. You'll see. I'm not even gonna do any tricks about this chapter even though there is probably some people that say I should do it causa kids read this and causa what's gonna be in it. But fuck that. This is a real true part and anybody can handle it. This is the way true things work OK. I know that's a bad swear again and maybe it will hafta come out but this part is not coming out and there's gonna be no tricks about it OK.

After dinner we go downstairs into the basement to watch a movie. But wait before we go downstairs Cass takes me all round her house and even into her bedroom for a minute while her parents do the dishes. This whole going around the house is probably not what you think of usually. I mean her

48

house is like as big as her lawn. It's huge. My whole house could practically fit right into her bedroom. There are lots of rooms we go into that I don't even know what they are for and she doesn't either rooms with couches and nothing else.

During this walking around and specially in her bedroom I find out alotta the stuff I had planned to ask her about to learn more about her. For one thing she went to Paris like one hundred times. I mean I didn't have that question in my plans or anything but it's one important thing I learned. She has pictures everywhere of her and her parents in Paris. She even has some of her and this one young guy in Paris and when I ask her about those ones she just says right out that it was a sorta boyfriend she had there but that it was just for when she was there. I thought OK she is a lot more like a grownup person than I really expected of her.

This acourse got alotta of the other information on her out right away. She's seventeen already if you can believe it and she plays just about every sport there is. She doesn't just play em but is actually like professional level good at em. She's a senior and already has actual Collegial Scholarships everywhere to play sports. Soccer is her big one and she says she'll either go to private schools somewhere east or something or State if she doesn't want to go too far.

I say to her State is good and I think it musta sounded kinda sad or something causa she just kisses me some in her room right there which is nice. It's a good thing about the kissing too causa I'm just starting to wonder whether it's a problem for me being at my level and her at her level. I tell her right then that we are only a year apart but two grades really and she says acourse she knew it all along and it's nothing. *True phew.*

OK so by the time we actually get to the part about going downstairs into the basement Cass's parents are already done doing the dishes as you can imagine causa the house is probably bigger than the Taj McHall Palace or whatever and it took us like two hours to go around it. A funny thing I actually said that part about the Taj McHall Palace out loud while we walk around and Cass laughs so hard snot sprays right outta her nose onto her face. And she is not embarrassed about it at all. But she just laughs out loud some more even when I laugh at her causa her snot and she just pulls up her little shirt and wipes it off right onto her shirt. True just like that. That's not like alotta the girls I know at all. Even when she pulls her shirt up I see her whole belly and part of her bra for a sec and you can imagine what this does to all my feelings I talked about earlier.

So we go down into the basement which was a door right on the kitchen and her parents are standing there in the kitchen leaning onto each other and they just watch us go. They both smile and everything but I'm not sure what they were watching us for exactly so I say thanks anyway for dinner and I smile back at em.

The basement is as big as the rest of the Taj McHall Palace acourse. It's carpet everywhere and in one part there are like a hundred leather couches bunched around the kinda TV you might expect to see in a Taj McHall Palace. Which is a really really big one.

So Cass pulls me all around the basement by my hand and then she throws down a bunch of huge Taj McHall Palace pillows and a blanket on the carpet right close in front of the TV. She doesn't ask me anything about what I want to watch but she just goes and puts a movie on right away. She says it's her dad's movie but that it's perfect for me right now causa a what's happened to me. So I think the worst of it abouta dad movie and I get ready for holding my eyeballs awake with some sporks or something for the next coupla hours. But here's the funny thing it's really kinda good if you can believe it.

We go down under the blanket to watch the movie and there are big pillows everywhere and Cass curls all up onto me while we watch and she even puts her hand under my shirt on my stomach while we watch. I can't remember what the movie is called now or anything causa what happened to my brains but it's about detention and nothing else at all really if you can believe it. And it's true good. Also I tell Cass that I think there's alotta dealin in this movie and we hafta stop the movie for a while so I can finally tell her all about my plans and ways of dealin. She says my dealin is pretty good but warns me some more that dealin usually can have some bad stuff happen about it. I say I know look at my face. And that gets us laughing which goes to more kissing.

OK I shouldn't a said that part about my brain but Mrs. H. says to leave it as that kinda thing goes into stories sometimes. So OK it stays til more on that part later obviously. But I do remember everything else about that whole night and I will never ever forget it. *True permanent.*

Then this gets better in acoupla different ways. First we stop the movie for me to talk on dealin and get this she asks me if I wanna beer. I tell her no that I felt kinda bad about not legally remembering every part of last time we were together in the bathtub. But she goes back into this other room and gets a bottle a beer and we split it anyway. So OK good and then we go back over everything that happened in the tub that night and we get most of it put back together by working over it together. She says she doesn't normally do that sorta thing with beer but that one of her sports volleyball maybe was over and all the girls went out for it. See Cass's friend D on the team knows Laura who's also Pup's friend where the party was. I tell her honest I do that sorta crap with the beer all the time and she says it's OK.

Then we finish the movie and we laughed a lot during most of it and we even split another beer til it was over. After we go back to lots more kissing and Cass really kisses me everywhere all over my body and I mean it. I sorta learn from it and do the same thing to her everywhere and then there is more things. Well I hafta say that I am not legally in place to do the Shake Spear Love Poem words for what is going on. And I thought about it too and this is not something that Mrs. H. told me to do it's my own decision. I'm just not gonna tell you exactly what happened that's all. Causa it's really just for me and Cass to know about. But I do want to say enough about it so you can get how true perfect it is. So I just hafta hope that you know it causa your own experiences. Or that one time in your life you will know it and then say oh yeah that was what he was talking about then in the basement with Cass. *True night.* So I'll just say that we did true Shake Spear Love Poems and I mean a lot too and and then we just went quiet and fell asleep right there on the basement floor.

9

OK so I freak some when the sun just starts to shine down into the basement barely. I mean I didn't try to sleep over at Cass's house but I did and I think that it's trouble for her causa her parents. But my brain is not broken so bad that I can't think about some things and I think about the beers and the Paris boy while she sleeps still next to me and I watch her and I guess it's probably OK.

She wakes up right then and we do a Shake Spear Love Poem though I should probably not a told you about that one at all. I tell her I hafta get my mom her crappy ole Ford Taurus back causa she goes to the town clerk's office early to do some other things before she starts her legal job there. Cass says OK to it and she walks me all the way upstairs and outta the wooden screen porch door and down the steps and we go really really slow across the lawn and I am true thankful for the big lawn that morning. We say goodbye forever with me in the car and her standing next to it til I finally hafta just cut it off so I can get my mom her car back.

My mom is standing on the porch with her purse and everything when I get back and I really thought I was in for it. I kinda drag my feet some in the gravel driveway to put off the yellin. Funny though she just stands there quiet as I come up and then she does the weirdest thing she just says nothing and put her arms around me and hugs me.

"How's Cass Joseph?" she asks after she hugs me for a long time and is just starting to let go a me.

"True, mom, true," I say looking at her.

"You are all bruises and scrapes Joseph," she says feeling and looking all over my face and stuff but not in the same way like Cass did it obviously, "but I bet you're feeling a lot better now aren't you?"

"True," I say with a big smile.

"Oh Joseph. I remember it. It heals everything." She kinda looks up into the sky dreamy for a sec like she's watching something up there or maybe looking for rain. "At least I think I remember it." Then the dreaminess goes all outta her face.

"Does it stay true like this?" I ask in a really stupid sounding voice.

She smiles and then makes a big frown almost like a clown might when he's talking to a dog or a baby or something. "No Joseph. It's never quite the same later on." She musta saw me frown too or probably more likely look like a goddamn ghost causa she smiles real big again then grabs me and hugs me really violent like and funny this time. "It's always like that

Joseph. Always. It's just...it's just a little bit less each time."

She pats me on the shoulder real hard acoupla times and then she actually hops down the steps like some kinda kangaroo or something. I never saw her do anything like that before. Then she jumps in the car and tears off almost knocking down the mailbox as she goes. I feel my shoulder where she hit me causa it still hurts there some and I think maybe my mom was dealin on me. Maybe I'm a sorta Holton Bolton for her.

I go back to bed and sleep for a while. Well that's a true bare lie acourse I just laid there awake for several hours and thought a little bit about what mom said but I gave it up causa the other thing to think about was so good and big I just wanted to do that for as long as I can.

Eventually I get up and clean up somewhat and put on some nicer but not special clothes and then I do probably the stupidest thing you'll ever hear of a kid doing who is suspended. I wait til about an hour before school let out time and then I walk the other way down the road to Memorial. Yes you heard me right I went to school on my suspended day from school. Just not my school but to Memorial instead. You can probably guess what I was planning now that you know some about how my dealin works especially when you get to the higher up levels of dealin like when I got to the part of making it right with Holton as I was telling you. Acourse nothing takes you up to the higher levels of dealin quite like

56

Shake Spear Love Poems do. *True right to the higher level dealin.*

So I have it in my plans to go to Memorial at let out time just to see what I can see of those Memorial guys. My deal this time is to say thanks for the tub stuff that's all. Kinda like the other high level dealin part was to say sorry to Holton that's all. The high level dealin is pretty much the simplest. It's all the things in the way of high level dealin that make it hard to actually get to it. I think about it a lot with the parts of my brain that still work and I figure that it's causa what they did in the bathtub with me and the water that it went straight to what happened next with Cass. It's sorta like the Third Fig Newton Law. Without the Memorial guys maybe all this true Cass stuff woulda never a happened.

I really hope you are kinda starting to see my high level dealin and this Third Fig Newton Law between the Memorial guys and Cass. There's a sorta connection between things like it but it's possible you don't see it. Especially if you are anything like these kids around here whose brains are already all broken apart on their own without even getting a smashin like me. Mrs. H. says that this part has to come out. She says I can't talk this way to you so you might not actually see this.

Anyway I stand there in the shade of a tree on a small patch of grass outside of Memorial for a while shaking my shirt somewhat to dry out all the sweat from the walk. There are blooms of something on the tree and they are pink and I can smell em whenever the breeze blows em around. I got there pretty early before let out which was good causa all the sweat. You already know all about that. Everybody there looks at me somewhat funny too. Not like flames of fire eyes like my school before but somewhat funny. I guess it makes sense if a strange guy with a smashed up face stands like an idiot under a tree at your school true you'd look at him funny. Acourse eventually some old Monky guy walks right up to me and asks me if I need help or stuff.

I just say to him thanks very much for checking on me but that I'm fine here and I'm waiting to meet some buddies of mine after school. Then I say to him it's a nice breeze for waiting. He was super happy with that what I said or the way I said it causa he was probably worried I was a pervert or burglar or something. I see on his face too that he really wants to ask me about my smashed up face but he doesn't do it. Here is a good example of being able to do stuff you want if you can just talk a little bit or say anything as I was saying.

The Monky guy is a sorta old guy and he has on one of those fancy dog collars that church people wear around their necks and he wears a big old gray sweater too and I notice that for sure. I mean I know old people are always super cold but really this old guy was only part way old and it was like burning hot out. So why was he wearing a sweater anyway? I know better than to ask him about it though.

The bell rings and almost every single kid in the world comes out and leaves before the guys that I am looking for come out acourse. They come out together and they are all there I think but maybe one or two are missing but I can't remember em that good anyway obviously. They look true different from the party too which surprises me somewhat. They look nice and setup for school and everything but their hair and clothes are not done as proper and straight and nice as they were at the party.

They stop all of em and stand looking at me for a while but then they come right over and introduce theirselves to me. They say they know all about what happened to me and everything in the shower and stuff and they even ask me some questions about it but not too many questions that it's stupid or weird. They say they are sorry for me and I say thank you for the water in the tub and they say sure and everything and they laugh a little bit about that. It's not exactly a good laugh and I see that they are not sure at all if I am up to something strange talking about the water or the tub.

So I hafta explain about Cass and even a little bit of my plans and some parts of high level dealin and I even get all the way up to the third Fig Newton Law stuff before I stop. They look at each other sideways and then they are quiet for a real long time. But then they break outta it and true laugh and they even hit me on the shoulder some which actually kinda hurt causa that was another smashed place. True I think I'm becoming more a Holton Bolton every minute.

It goes quiet after that so I know it's time to move out good soon. So I invite em to come by my house sometime for a beer. I tell em all about these other plans I have about beers and how it all works and they were pretty excited to come by and see it going. I would tell you some on that but there may be true Sherlock Interpol legal problems for me if I do Mrs. H. says so I'll leave it out.

I get outta there and take my time walking back causa I'm suspended anyway and I do not even have a shift at the hardware store. The rest of the day is quiet and everything and even Cass comes over to my house late acourse causa her sports and she eats with me and my mom though legally my mom had already eaten and she just sits with us and talks and stuff. Me and Cass we hang out really late together but I'm not gonna tell you anything about it causa it's pretty covered already on that area of things. Cass doesn't true sleep over but leaves sometime super late on account a getting up for sports before the sun peaks out.

That is pretty much the last real quiet nice day for a while. My suspension is over. I go back to school and things are a little different or something. I'm not sure how to get it to you what the air was like at school other than by saying that the air was thick with alotta the things that have been happening. And sometimes when there's alotta things happening in the air it sorta just blows up. Kinda like what Mr. Cooper told us about in social studies with the Rodney King Angeles stuff and somewhat with the Detroit Motor Burning Riots and even that Kent Vietnam State killing. Sometimes stuff gets into the air where it can't get out but by blowing up. Let's just say it is in the air when I go back to school for sure.

So we got the tempest or tornado or whatever blustering around in the air and the flames of fire in all the eyeballs are there again and the fires are really ready to spread for true it looks. I'll tell you more about it in the next chapter causa it kinda needs it's own place to start and everything. Also this is partway through everything so it's probably a good place to stop off and go to sleep if you are looking for that place. I know I'm always doing that.

10

OK this chapter is gonna hafta be both a Duck Duck Goose first and then a Grand Central Station right after it causa that's just how it has to work out. So hopefully no one of you needs to skip both of those kinda parts so you at least get some of it to keep going on.

OK Duck Duck Goose first. Before I get to what bad happened at school this morning I'm gonna tell you acoupla quick things about the boring stuff like phones this time. You probably started to have this idea already about me being a crazy person but this part of it is probably gonna make it explode wide open the lid on how crazy you think I am.

I don't have a phone OK that's it. Now you might expect some kinda long things for me to say about why but I'm not. Some things in life are just true simple that's all. I don't like phones is one of em. I can buy one if I want obviously causa the hardware store but I just don't like talkin on em that's all. I don't even like the regular old style phones like the one at my house. When it rings I just ignore it. My mom yells sometimes at me about it but I just ignore that too.

The only other thing about this I learned now with Cass is that it makes plans with her more twisted and it takes more work. But really you know about me and plans and that is one thing I can do really good so we figure it out. It mostly just takes plans in advance of when we are gonna do stuff. OK she also calls my house and talks to my mom about it sometimes. Funny my mom never yelled at me once even about these calls from Cass even though she used to when I ignored the phone.

Now really I'm sure this Duck Duck Goose thing about the phones seems true stupid to you but you will see in a sec why it goes into some of the things coming up. OK let that last Duck Duck Goose be the one for you to start again reading if you're skipping the boring parts causa now I gotta start going into the next parts of actual stuff going on.

Cass gets me in her car really super early that morning which was pretty nice of her causa she has already been up and doing a sports thing for acoupla hours. She hasn't even showered yet and she's all sweaty driving the car into school and I think about how things are really switched around with us about sweating today. I mention it about the sweating to her and she doesn't even hear it she's staring off and her face looks kinda serious. That's when she tells me some of the things she saw and heard at school already in the dark early this morning.

Apparently there is big crowds of people with signs and everything already in the morning darkness all lined up at the very edge of the school property. There are so many people that there's camera news people out there talking to em and making the news. I ask if it's about me and what happened in the shower and she says it's partly but it's also abouta assembly thing that one of the school groups is planning for this AM.

See I missed all about the assembly thing causa I was suspended and all for what happened to me. Cass says that when I was gone some of the groups like theater kids and counselors got together and planned to put on a assembly about the rights of all peoples and it was real clear causa they made up and advertised with big signs everywhere at the school. It is real clear about gays lesbians and trans peoples too so no one can mistake it. So this is how the early flames of fire eyes that are already blustery get sparked into the big blow up I was talking about. There was the shower baboon circus with me in the middle of it and now this assembly and it true sparks the tensions and there's alotta grouping off of school kids. And now it's spread to the whole town says Cass. Now the whole damn town is apparently gathered around all angry on both sides right at the school.

"Joseph," Cass says to me with the real serious look on her face and her hands sweating onto the steering wheel, "to be safe you really need to keep to yourself today. I think there is going to be trouble and

I don't want you in the middle of it again. I want you safe."

"OK OK Cass." I smile at her and I kinda like the way she is all caring about me. But I gotta admit I'm worried some about the serious look on her face especially causa she's told me stuff like this before and she sorta knows about things like it and it always sorta happens what she says. "I think I got the worst part behind me mostly." Acourse saying it then sounded all real good but it's in fact one of the most not true things that I ever said in my life so far.

"If you can...please keep quiet if someone says something unfair to you. I know it will be hard for you...but I think it is the best way." She looks at me with those serious grownup like eyes some more.

I don't say OK OK right away and I turn the gears over it in my head making some small little plans on how I might do this thing she is asking. But then I think I got it, "OK OK Cass but will you sit with me at the assembly anyway? That will make it easier."

"Yes Joseph of course. The assembly is right after first period. I'll meet you at your locker." She looks a lot less serious after that thankfully. "Oh. Maybe you should take it easy in gym first period and skip the shower."

"OK OK Cass." I don't need to do any plans small or big before I say OK on that one.

OK Grand Central Station coming pretty much right after the assembly gets out as you are probably already thinking something like that. Cass and me we sit kinda near the doors right on the far left most side of the big old theater or auditorium or whatever and it's packed super full of kids everywhere. There are teachers everywhere too walking and checking on everything. It's super rowdy at first but there is shushing and even some yelling and detentions by the teachers and it calms sorta and goes dark.

The assembly acting show stuff is not half bad really. I wanna tell this one small funny thing that happened before I go onto the bad part. During the talking on stage in the dark theater Cass kinda touches my arm and hands and neck some and she makes some nice whispers to me about how she likes me the way I am. Then she gets yelled at for talking right in the middle of everybody. She turns red as a red beet or whatever on her face and I see true that this sorta thing has never happened to her before. I laugh a little bit at her but real quiet to not make it worse for her and I think she finally learned some things from me instead of the other way around.

OK enough the bad part starts as we get outta the theater place or auditorium. Cass and me we get out almost first and we walk kinda quick down the hall away from it all. We're talking about how we kinda actually liked the things they did and said on stage and how it might make the school kids at least turn the corner more on the whole thing.

But acourse the corner isn't turned at all as you'll see but it's going right back to where it started. Right then some big sports lady yells DIKE in the crowd coming out. I only know it's a sports lady causa Cass says her name right away. I think she says Bell or something like that. Apparently Bell yelled DIKE to this other sports lady which is supposed to be her friend. I think this girl's name is Di or Liz. Well Di or Liz really just punches this Bell right in her face and knocks her over. And I say right away that Bell really oughta not say that kinda thing to someone who can punch her in the face so good. But then I remember I'm supposed to keep my mouth shut on this thing.

Cass grabs my arm hard with both her hands as if she already knows what's coming but then Bell is not done at all and she grabs onto Di or Liz's legs and bites right onto her like some kinda dog. Then it all goes bad at once. Like one hundred girls or more maybe tear and scratch and punch and bite and pull bloody hair right outta heads. And it's not just sports girls now too but a bunch a others. It's true bad chaos. It's chaos so bad that as I said before to get to this part that no one even takes any pictures or movies with their phones which is exactly what always happens in these things as I'm sure you know. Instead kids are using their phones to bash in other peoples heads and they're even throwing em at each other.

Kids throw and hit with books too and whatever they have really. And then all of a sudden there are boys in there too fighting on each other. Then the boys even fight on the girls too if you can believe it. I guess that part is what really does it for me when I see one guy a kinda creep I know about already he stabs this girl in the legs with a pencil and this girl howls like a wolf and practically scratches the eyeballs right outta this guys face and head.

So I run right into it acourse that's how stupid I am. I don't even know how I got myself free of Cass's grasping causa she was like true clung to me. But I did it and some of the worst of it when it was all done was the scratches on my arms from Cass and not from all the other bad stuff. I go right to the girl who was scratching this guy's face off and I am meaning to help her out some or something with the creep guy and that's when it happens. This phone that was part metal and that was kinda already broken off twirls right through the air and smacks me right in my other eye. Not the black eye but the good one if you can believe it. True at this point you could probably guess this sorta smashing was coming just for me.

Anyway I kinda go down on my hands and knees right there and hold my eye which is bleeding pretty bad. If it's OK for me to skip ahead for you for one sec I will. One good thing about this is I don't go blind or anything from it and I do end up OK after this smashing and I eventually see pretty clear with my eye again. You'll find out more on that area later so don't worry. And now acourse you see that all the boring stuff about phones earlier was just so you can see how strange it is for me to get my eye smashed by a phone. That and how true bad it is causa everybody is using their phones to try to kill each other instead a taking pictures. Mrs. H says this is the good sorta thing to go in here but I don't know it sounds boring to me still.

So the teachers are all making their way into this fire or blustering but they aren't making too great a progress against it yet. But they do get some progress on it soon and I don't think it's really causa the teachers in there but mostly just causa so many kids are true hurt and can't fight any more.

Well it's just then at this part causa I see a flash of it through my blood hands with my good eye that the Bell girl gets stomped in the head. This is really why it's a Grand Central Station part to remind you if you might puke or something. Anyway it's Di or Liz's brother who does it. Di or Liz is down and out bad at this part by Bell and Di or Liz's brother goes crazy on it and goes onto Bell and beats her bad til she is down too. Then he stomps her in the head before the teachers can get all the way in there. The Grand Central Station thing is that Bell never did get up and later she died from it. It makes my stomach sick even writing it now causa I saw it happen with my one good eye.

I know you might think I'm gonna say more about Bell getting some things she asked for since it's her who did it all really in the beginning. But I won't do it even though I kinda feel like it. I say true stupid things all the time everyday as you know but I won't do that on Bell causa now she is dead and that is bad enough.

One other girl Jessica died too but not til much later on like seven months. I did not see that one at all but they said she got cut in a big vein or something and lost too much blood so that she went into a coma for a long time. Then they said her brain was dead and her parents had to pull the plug on her and she died then.

Di or Liz was in a coma too but she did come back from it and went back to school eventually though she was done with sports apparently. Cass even got hurt but just a minor bit causa she jumped on me after and kinda kept me from getting kicked on more when I was all bent over with my eye. She was right back to her sports though so that is really good.

The other part about this riot at school is that when they started pulling the kids out by the cops and ambulances the whole riot started up again with the grownups outside with the signs. I don't see that one at all causa by this time I am on a stretcher with practically my entire head wrapped up in bandages. But people say it was bad too. Good thing though is that cops are a lot better at doing the riots than teachers so no one died out there. The worst of it was the kids inside.

You probably guessed but even our town's moron Sherlock Interpols finally had to arrest a bunch of people on this one. I mean people died and everything right? So Di or Liz's brother pretty much got the worst of it later on as it was obvious he was trying to legally slaughter Bell. He ended up going to grownup jail for pretty much the rest of his life. Some other kids got put in kid jail too but on lesser legal slaughtering and they were all out pretty quick. A funny part is that none of the grownups got arrested from the grownup riot. This is probably something that mighta helped with what came later but who knows for sure.

OK Grand Central Station. I'm gonna stop telling more details about it causa really you all know it was all true bad. Two people actually died which is about as bad as it gets at the high school level before you get to the Africa level of things like this. Also just so you know I do believe that there are no funny things in a true bad situation like this so don't take some things I say later to mean it. It's just that there are some parts that sorta came outta it that I hafta talk about later in a funny way. I also put that last thing in here so you don't think this whole story is just bloody smashing all the time. It may help if you need that stuff to go on with it.

11

So instead of just local news peoples at the school like before after the riot there are true nation news peoples all over town everywhere and even at my house. These Dan Kenneth Rathers knock on my door day and night causa somehow it got out what happened in the shower with me. Alotta peoples get it in their brains that I am the epic center or the start of it. I don't hear any of it myself but Cass's dad tells me that some of it's good causa some of the really big Dan Kenneth Rathers say that the school peoples made a huge mistake by not taking care of the shower stuff in the right way.

I didn't ever talk to the Dan Kenneth Rathers not even once unless you count this thing as talking. I have a reason or plans about this if you wanna hear it. See one thing I noticed about Dan Kenneth Rathers is that they are always true dealin always. They are never not dealin. And I don't mean kid dealin like I do but real grownup darkness dealin. The kinda dealin where part of you goes bad if you do it too much.

Anyway I don't wanna risk it talking to em causa as you already know I have some weaknesses or bad habits when it comes to dealin.

OK Mrs. H. talked to me about something that I oughta put in here. There are these older type nation news peoples that are not always dealin apparently. I think she said maybe Studs Newsie Terkels or some such peoples. Anyway according to Mrs. H. they do good things too and not just dealin. Good enough things that the whole idea of this country's foundation would crumble without em causa they are a fourth state pole or leg that holds us up or something. OK you can blame Mrs. H. for getting that Duck Duck Goose stuff in here not me. At any rate I never talked to any of em good or bad.

What I do is just walk straight past all the Dan Kenneth Rathers to Cass's car. We drive all kinda backwards ways to her house and that works for a while but they eventually find us. Thing is that it's still way better at Cass's causa as you know the Taj McHall Palace is so far from the street causa green Antarctica that you can never really hear em talk talk talk. Even mom comes over and spends alotta nights in her own guest room at Cass's for a while. It's creepy at first all of us together but eventually it's nice. Also Cass's dad is real good about dealin with Dan Kenneth Rathers.

Well besides the Dan Kenneth Rathers going nuts over the whole town the rest of the town just goes quiet for a few days. What would you expect when people actually die but to go quiet? Acourse a few of the true church nutters still blabber on with their signs and stuff but those people don't care about deaths or anything those types just wanna shout angry at bad people all the time no matter what.

I'm let outta the hospital the next day in fact causa it's just a medium bad cut on my eyeball. I got another great big black eye outta it and I hafta wear a white bandage forever and then a black patch after that too. So basically I look like the biggest idiot arg pirate patch and practically my whole face and body are covered with bruises and cuts. I think about gettin a bird talker for my shoulder or something to kinda go full arg pirate patch but not really. Still I mention the bird talker to Holton.

Holton Bolton loves it acourse. I get back to the hardware store right away after I get outta the hospital causa I like it and it keeps the mail books coming in. It's awkward at first causa Holton Bolton and his family are kinda on the other side of the war going. But I was practically killed already twice and look bad as hell too so Mr. Bolton just mumbles some and lets me back into work. So thankful true the old Boltons aren't the nutter blubbers that wanna just yell at bad people as I was saying about. Acourse Holton is still hangering on with those circus baboons but he doesn't really understand what's going on as I said and we get along just fine especially causa I look like I do smashed up.

It get so I can get Holton Bolton practically peeing in his pants by counting out my bruises and cuts and scrapes and telling him the stories about em.

I don't know why at all but I even tell funny stories around almost getting stick ass raped and Holton sometimes shoots snot outta his nose at that. It's like I said before some funny things hafta come outta it. Outta everything really. True though I think Holton and I are the only two people laughing in the whole town these days.

There is a funeral soon after for Bell and I end up actually going causa Bell was on a sports team with Cass. Cass and her were not close and the team they were on together was in a different season then but still you go to funerals causa it I guess. It's true sad as you can imagine. Her mom and dad are just complete melted in tears and heaving and even some screaming. *True tragedy ladies*. But a man maybe her uncle says some nice words on Bell and I even learn that her true name was Mabelle or Mabel or something.

One hard part about the funeral is that the super angry circus baboon Jeff is actually there. Turns out he is a cousin to Bell which makes some sense if you think about what Bell yelled at the beginning. It's like Jeff woulda done. His face is healed up mostly but it's still a big huge scar mark right on his cheek where I chewed him that makes him look even more crazy and mean than before.

He is wearing a suit which looks about as outta place on him as it would on an actual real live baboon. He does not say one word to me or to anybody at all really but he does stare me down super mean and true crazy for a while in the middle of the whole thing. Cass sees it too and pulls hard on my arm again which kinda hurts causa where she pulled on me there at the riots. I shoulda known by this crazy staring that Jeff was not done on me at all and sure enough you'll see about that part later on in this.

OK so it's a real good time for Cass and me for a while between all these bad things. Causa I stay at her house all the time we have alotta time together especially in the car in the morning going to school together and then again late at night after her practices. We even start reading the same books together which is nice causa it's one place where we are really alike. Not that I should tell you about it but I think I even get pretty good at Shake Spear Love Poems causa this time too.

This reminds me that there is one more Duck Duck Goose thing I need to add real quick. It's real small I promise. I don't really know the legal way to put this here so I'll just say it. Not all the stuff in here is true *true*. I mean all these things really did happen and I am real and Cass is real and our Shake Spear Love Poems are true real. But still this story thing has to stop at some time and my real life has to go on and then some stuff happens much later afterwards that sorta changes some of the things in here a little bit. It doesn't make em *not* true really I mean it just sorta changes em a little tiny bit and makes em just a tiny bit different than what they seem in here if you can understand it. But I still can't change any of it causa I hafta put it true like it was at the time and not later. True hard to say it so it makes sense so I'll just leave it. OK Duck Duck Goose.

OK so I start going to Cass's soccer games too. Even Pup and Pete go to one with me which is like acoupla dogs playing cards or something outta whacked like that art poster. It's about the only time I see em since the whole thing started. Since Cass I don't find much reason to drink beers with em in Pup's back woods like before. They think the soccer is boring but at least they go.

They are important games for Cass causa she is one of the main important players and they are going on through towards winning state for like a dozen times in a row. That is mostly why Cass has gotten all those scholarships. I really like going to the games causa it gives me a chance to watch Cass doing something real good and something that makes her happy. It does take me a little bit to get used to soccer but now I'm all up on it.

You probably will never in a million years believe it but I was already kinda into sports. I mean not soccer obviously causa it's not a real sport at least in this country. But I did play soccer myself when I was young and I played almost all the other sports too but then I just sorta drifted away from playing em as high school came on. I still watch alotta sports though on TV and stuff. Football is the big one for me really. Football is pretty big around here for everyone on account a state college. I like it when fall comes on and the leaves turn and football is on.

Believe it or not my mom actually takes me up to state college every year so we can watch a football game at the big ole stadium there. I mean she doesn't really know or care about football but she likes the campus city causa that's where she went. So every fall we go and I watch the football and she just sits around during it talking to me some and then we do some stuff around campus city that she wants to do. Usually that means lunch or dinner at this dirty ole bar restaurant where there's peanut shells everywhere and kinda good burgers. It's a nice place that I think's been around since the dinosaurs and it's mostly some crazy old guys in there but also some young kids too drinking beer and doing dates.

I'm pretty sure it's a important place for things that happened to my mom when she was in school here. She always has this happy look on her face when we eat there. I keep waiting for her to tell me about what sorta happened to her here but she never says. I can just ask I know but she has some bad stuff too that happened to her so I just wait and maybe she'll tell me sometime if she wants to. If we sit for too long and quiet at lunch then I just talk about the game and other things and that works OK.

When I tell Cass about the ole bar restaurant and peanuts and the burgers at state college town she says it sounds super nice. She says if she chooses state college we can do our dates there too. True plan I tell her.

Cass says one thing about state college town is that they aren't doing the warring and blustering that our town is now doing about different people. She says they already mostly done with their wars way back and are past it now. Now different peoples at state college war less or at least about smaller or different things. I say I can't wait til our town is way past it too. Cass tells me I might be gone from town before it's past here and I hope she's wrong. True Cass is probably never wrong about stuff like this though as you know already.

OK so this is pretty much a whole Duck Duck Goose chapter. Oh well like I said you probably needed a break from all the smashings. Also like I said it's also more smashings coming as you probably guessed.

12

Holton Bolton and I are pretty much best buds at the hardware store for a while as I said. We keep each other entertained or at least I keep him laughing mostly. The school stays pretty much quiet for awhile but there is still some bluster tension in the air. And like I said about that stuff in the air needs to blow up. Well we got our blow up already but it wasn't enough to get it all out apparently.

Then a funny thing happens at the store. Goat Ed comes back in and gets another giant box of nails. Acourse he stares at me like a ghost for abouta another hour. I ask again what he's building and I say it's gotta be something big with all these nails. He tells me again it's his dad doing it really. He's just helping.

After he left I tell Holton Bolton about how I went out to the Schmidts and looked at it a bit and saw Goat Ed getting it from his dad. Holton tells me Goat Ed's dad was one of the worst ones at the grownup riots that happened after at our school. He says he even got arrested that was news to me.

As Holton tells me this I remember about watching at the Schmidts and I start wondering where this thing is that Goat Ed's dad is building with all these nails. I mean I saw Goat Ed go out back of his shack or whatever but I didn't see anything big getting built or anything. I mention this to Holton and he tells me that Goat Ed actually came in lots more times and got lots more nails especially when I was away in the hospital.

OK so this gets my Sherlock Interpol hat on and I start working on it in my brains. Holton is no good for this sorta thing and he just stares at me like he's a big floating pig or something from that parade in New York Town on Thanksgiving when I tell him my ideas about it. So instead I tell Cass my ideas on this Goat Ed and his nails and she gets pretty scared looking.

"Joseph." She holds my hands after she says it and squeezes it hard as hell so I know something probably serious is coming. "I want you to stay away from Ed Peterson and his dad. I saw Mr. Peterson at school when we were taking you out to the ambulance. I think he's dangerous."

"OK OK Cass." She's got me spooked some about Goat Ed's dad now but I can't just let off my ideas on the nails. "But about the nails Cass. I've been working at the hardware store for a real long time now and some contractors that build houses and stuff still come into there instead of those big places out by the mall and I pretty much know by now how much nails they need to build stuff."

She squeezes me hard still and it kinda hurts but I keep going, "He's buying more nails than he needs to build like five houses. Something big. If he's building something big we should at least see some part of it somewhere around that shack they live in."

After I left off talking Cass just stares at me forever without saying anything. Her eyes grow sorta big like they do sometimes when she's gonna cry but she doesn't actually cry. "Ok Joseph." She thinks for like a million more minutes staring right at me with those big eyes. "After soccer tomorrow night. I'll drive us out there and we'll park at that spot you told me about in the trees and take a look."

"OK OK Cass," I say.

"But only if you promise me you will not get outta the car. Promise me you will not go anywhere near Ed or Mr. Peterson."

"OK OK Cass. I promise." After I say it I sorta peel her hands off a me where they were digging into my skin.

So it takes us a long time after Cass gets home before we actually make it out to the spot in the trees we talked about. It's the first part of the night just after the sun sets when there's still some light in the sky. We sit quiet in the car with the windows rolled down watching carefully all over the Schmidts place. There is nothing to see at all. There is a light on in the shack but no moving around anywhere inside that we can see.

Some of the goats come outta the big barn then they sorta chew around the pen and they go back in.

The little tanker trucks crawl around spraying and one actually dusts up the little road behind the big house and then it comes in and parks next to the big barn. Two guys get out and pull acoupla big empty plastic looking barrels down off the back of the little tanker truck and roll em into the big barn.

We watch all of this like true Sherlock Interpols for a long time without saying a word. But then nothing happens for the longest time and we get back to talking quiet instead. Cass says she likes the smell of the pine needles that are laying everywhere all around the car. I say I like the creaking sound the trees make when the wind kicks up a bit. The wind kicks up only the tiniest bit but causa it's a little bit towards night it's an almost cool breeze that comes into the car. It feels good. I kiss her then and it's real nice even though it makes us forget our reason for coming and it probably makes us bad Sherlock Interpolers. We stay parked in the trees for a long time kissing before we give up and go back to Cass's.

We come back the next night a little later causa Cass's soccer practice goes super late and Cass has to shower and eat after she gets back. We watch as the black night comes on and then Cass puts on some music pretty quiet in the car. Music is one of the things that's more Cass's but I am getting up on it too. She plays me every kinda music you can imagine and not just popular kid's stuff. She plays me a super ole French lady stuff from her time in Paris. She also plays me some dusty ole music with banjos and those fiddler things. She even always plays me stuff based kinda on things I said to her before which is pretty weird and nice and so you know she must really listen to alotta music to do it.

That night she plays me a ole John Hookey song or something based on a thing I told her about our school burning. The Detroit Motor Burning Riots that I also told you about already and I say this one sounds perfect for what is going on at our school and town and Cass agrees. Then we let the music go out and then we kiss some in the darkness. We watch the shack some bits too when we remember but nothing happens so we go home.

We do this parking in the trees for alotta more nights and each night we watch less and kiss more and just sit and listen to the music quiet in the dark. Turns out it's just a nice way to be together without sports or dinner or homework or the hardware store in the way. Those are some of my favorite times I spent with Cass when I remember it even though what happened next was bad.

OK so I'm gonna give you a kinda early Grand Central Station for the bad thing that's coming down here in awhile. It's one of those things that happens every now and then in the world and it's bad and also all over the news. It's probably happened where you saw it on the news or been somewhere near it. If you were actually really near it then this part coming on may trauma you so you may want to skip it. I don't wanna be the one to bring all that stuff up for you if it's bad for you OK. Just look for Grand Central Station when it's done like normal.

So on about the tenth night or so of our Sherlock Interpoling and kissing in the trees we're just about to drive off when finally we see something happen. The big Schmidt house is all dark this time and the whole farm is pretty still like for the whole time we're there. There's no tanker trucks or nothing dusting up the roads. There is one light on in the little crappy shack but we don't see anything for a long time and we're just about to go when we see it. The front shack door swings open kinda rough and out comes Goat Ed and then Mr. Peterson who's yelling at Ed acourse but in a kinda quiet yelling voice sorta way. We see Ed clear enough causa his dad's got this big ole flashlight shining around the dark.

Mr. Peterson yells at Ed some more and Ed gets into the crappy ole van and starts it up. Mr. Peterson walks around behind the house and we lose sight of him blocked by the shack but we see the big ole light ray from his flashlight spraying light all around the green sod grass. Then we hear a big metal slamming sound and I say to Cass that he musta opened up the ole Wizard of Oz cellar door.

Cass looks at me with her big scared eyes and what's going on at Goat Ed's shack gives me some goosestuff too. Then Ed actually turns the van around and drives right across the lawn around to the backside of the crappy shed. Then we hear that little dinger that some trucks or vans make so Ed musta be backing up the van to the Wizard of Oz door.

After just a little bit more the van door creaks and then slams closed and then the spraying light from

Mr. Peterson's flashlight disappears. They musta gone into the basement says Cass. The whole top of the shack was all washed out in red from the backside car lights. Then we hear some strange kinda noises like scrapes and thuds and some yelling by Goat Ed's dad. But we can't see any of it really blocked by the shack. So I says to Cass we need to drive on up the River Road a ways and see what we can see looking back.

Cass says OK if you can believe it and starts up the car but then I stop her. I better drive I say so she can look back and watch careful at the shack. I never could see too good at night and since the thing happened to my other eye I really can't see for shit at night at all. I mean it's still legal good enough for me to drive but not by much. She says OK and I get out and go around while the car's still running and she just slides right over to the passenger side.

I pull out onto the River Road with the car lights still turned dark and I only turn em on once we go a bit down the road. I drive real slow like way below the speed limit to give Cass a good chance to look on it. We creep and crawl along the River Road and I'm nervous as hell and once we get like almost a mile up the road it seems Cass leans almost all the way outta the window looking back at the shack.

"What is it Cass?" I say.

She pulls her head and her whole body back into the window and drops down into the seat and for a sec she just stares out the window and I think maybe she saw something bad. "They're loading a big white barrel into the back of the van Joseph. They're wearing respirators and they have on chemical suits I think."

"Oh shit Cass. We gotta call the Sherlock Interpols right away," I say to Cass in a super nervous whispering horse sorta voice.

"I didn't bring my phone Joseph." She still stares out the window for a second but then she gets herself together and turns to me. "Drive to my house Joseph. We'll tell my dad and he can call the police. He knows the Sheriff."

That's a good idea I tell Cass but I am kinda having a hard time seeing in the dark so as soon as we get far enough to make the first turn I pull over and we switch back places and Cass drives. The rest of the way Cass drives as fast as I ever saw her drive. I bump around the passenger seat pretty good knocking all my bruises.

Cass's dad is in his pajamas already but he is still awake and he calls the Sheriff right away and tells em what we saw at the Schmidt farm. The Sheriff guy says he'll send someone out to Cass's house tomorrow anyway to take a look or something but Cass's dad says to the Sheriff guy on the phone in a kinda loud voice that they hafta send someone out to the Schmidt farm right away. I think from the way that Cass's dad talks that he is a kinda important person and he must be causa he hangs up the phone after that and says the police are going to the Schmidt farm now to investigate.

13

This bad part doesn't take long to pretty much spin outta control from here. The Sheriff comes over to Cass's acourse and brings acoupla regular Sherlock Interpols and they Sherlock Interpol our whole story and they take it very serious with us and treat us nice I think causa Cass's dad is important. So these two Sherlock Interpols get everything down from us and it takes like two whole hours and they are about to leave when about eight more Sherlock Interpols come screaming up to Cass's house. They come across the big green dream lawn into the porch light in a real rush and talk to the Sheriff and Cass's dad outside where we can't hear em. Some of em have on uniforms but a couple have on just plain old suits.

Cass and I watch from inside causa we're kinda tired from all the talking to the Sherlock Intepols. Cass's dad comes in then and two of the uniform type cops come in after him and Cass's dad offers em something to drink but they say no. He tells em to make theirselves comfortable and they nod but they just stand there with their hands on their big ole belts with their guns and stuff which doesn't look very comfortable.

Then Cass's dad sits us both down on the couch and tells us that the Sherlock Interpols went to the Schmidt farm but the van and Goat Ed were already gone. But Mr. Peterson was there and he had a gun and shot at the Sherlock Interpolers when they tried to ask him some questions. One Sherlock Interpol was shot actually and was already in the hospital but he was gonna be OK probably. The other Sherlock Interpol was a lady and she shot Mr. Peterson then and he pretty much died right away there in his crappy ole shack.

Now they're out hunting for Goat Ed and the van and these two police are gonna stay here in the house and two more are gonna stay outside all night in case Goat Ed tries to come here.

Acourse Cass's dad says we should try to get some sleep but Cass has a million questions especially is there gonna be school tomorrow. Cass's dad says he doesn't know but he's gonna make some calls about that next. He tells us to try to get some sleep again so we go upstairs but acourse we can't do any sleeping at all with what's going on. Funny thing about that night is that Cass just says for me to come right into her room and not the guest room where I sometimes sleep. I mean I always sneak into her room after anyway but tonight there is no sneaking but only going right into her room. We lay there in her room on her bed in our full clothes and we just talk about it all night.

Eventually Cass's dad knocks quietly on the door and Cass goes and opens it a little but Cass's dad doesn't come in. He whispers to Cass out in the hall. Cass shuts the door and comes back to me and says that there is gonna be school tomorrow but that alotta cops will be there even the state cops are coming to help. We sleep a little bit then but not much and pretty soon it's morning.

Everybody in the house is up super early right as the sun is sparkling into the hundreds of windows all over the quiet Taj McHall Palace. So we eat breakfast super early causa we're already up. I guess it's a normal time for breakfast for Cass anyway causa she's always up for sports. That's when Cass's dad says they searched all night for the van but didn't find it. He says the search was moved out to three whole states for the white van but there has not been one single sight of it anywhere which is strange.

This makes Cass look at me with that scared look but then she has to go and I can see she doesn't want to. But she does go and that is one thing about Cass that I'm sure you can guess. She's really good at sports and some other things causa she's always going to em and doing em even when she doesn't want to. That's how you get real good at things I guess.

That's when I tell Cass I think I'm gonna walk to school since it's still like two hours til school actually starts and I can't sit here doing nothing. Cass says no acourse but I tell her that it's better for me to walk causa I think I know a way that I can stay away from the roads anyway.

This makes her think about it for a minute and I take this minute to ask her dad if there is a way I can cut out back of The Prentice and get to the ole McKenzie Dead Cement Factory. He says it's a few miles but he thinks there's probably a way and he says the whole back forest of The Prentice is owned by the Millers a few doors down and that he'll call em and ask if I can walk through. Then he says if I go straight north through their woods I hafta cut across the old Farm Road but I'll eventually come to a conservation thing where the Fish Pond is. From there it's a right turn and then a mile of fields or so to the ole McKenzie Dead Cement Factory.

I say I know it from there causa I used to run cross country freshman year. We ran all over the cross country trails in the woods just easta school and even some on the old burned out grounds of the ole McKenzie Dead Cement Factory. Acourse Cass says no and looks pretty serious again about it but I see the way she looks at me and it kinda makes sense causa how I look with one still mostly black eye and the other with the arg pirate patch.

"Joseph, I'll drive you to school," she says with a sorta final and done way about it.

"Cass I can't sit around school for two hours waiting for it to start. I'll go crazy," I say it sorta quiet.

"You can read Joseph," she says in a little bit less of a final way.

"Cass any other day and I'd do it but today I gotta get out around. I think I really need to walk a while before school starts."

Cass's dad comes to help me then and says that a walk might do me good even that he's gonna give his phone for me to take with me so Cass can call me anytime. That does it. She still gives me a longer than normal big hug before she goes and says for me to be careful and smart causa she has a bad feeling about today. Acourse she always has a bad feeling but still it probably legally means something bad is gonna happen as usual when she opens her mouth about it. And true it does.

So the Miller's say sure to me cutting through their woods and one of the uniform Sherlock Interpols walks me all the way to the end of the Prentice road before I say OK OK and she leaves me off there. The Dan Kenneth Rathers are all kept outta the whole development now so they can't see me going down to the Millers.

The sun is up and it's bright and warm already and I'm sweating some already causa my books and backpack are heavy. I get deep into the Miller woods and there's a dog barking some ways off and it's dark in there causa the sun can't really poke much through the leaves. Anyway it's nice and cool in the dark woods and that helps the sweat some and I go pretty fast through there. The ground is kinda wet and dark dirt and it smells really good in there for a woods and it's pretty quiet besides a few dog barks and I think it's the first time probably ever I don't hear a lawn mower going somewheres in the Prentice.

I get to the Farm Road a lot faster than I think and the Farm Road is deserted and I run right across it and jump up over a broken old barby fence into the conservation place like I'm in some kinda movie. *True Rambo Movie*. Then I walk in the conservation place for a while and I can't see the pond yet but I know it's straight ahead I think causa my mom used to take me here when I was little. It's just like I remember except the grass is super tall like all the way up to my chest and it's swaying around kinda in the light wind blowing.

Finally the grass gets smaller and there are a few huge trees just ahead like oakey trees or something and I know that it's the pond. Since I get there fast I decide to go left all the way round the pond instead of straight right around off toward school. Turns out the pond is more like a huge lake compared to what I remember it and it takes a lot longer than I think to go around. So I was sweating real good again by the time I get all the way around and start out toward the ole Mckenzie Dead Cement Factory.

I think I might be late for school but then I remember I have Cass's dad's phone and I check it and I still have forty minutes so that might be plenty of time. I get over the old broken barby fence easy again and leave the conservation place and then I'm walking on the cracked up and grassy ole cement road that used to be the back way into the ole McKenzie Dead Cement Factory. I know this part well causa I ran here all the time. The real cross country trails are in the woods that are part of school on the far side of the factory area. Pup and me but barely nobody else used to run all those trails and then cut out here and run on this old cement as well. It was pretty good running but you had to watch your steps on the cracks.

Mostly I just liked looking at the old crappy buildings falling apart that's why I ran here. The old huge tube that runs all the way across the building is even more broke down now but it's still there some like a big metal snake. I suddenly feel like running again causa I was used to it being nice here in this place so I start to run. That lasted about five minutes before I decide that it's a stupid thing causa I'm breathing so hard and I'm now true drenched in sweat. So I just walk again and hope the woods ahead is cool so I'm not all drenched and smelling like a horse or cow when I get to school.

I smile at that some causa my plans on dates in the summer and not smelling like a horse or cow or anything causa now I actually have all the dates I want and it true doesn't matter how I smell or anything. I make it to the woods super fast after that.

I walk up the first steep dirt path into the woods and it's slow causa my backpack and books and this woods is not dark and cool like the Millers. There's alotta light and the ground is torn up pretty good from all the runners and just kids doing stupid things in a woods by school as that's what kids always do in a woods by school. I walk for a long time upwards on the paths as the whole forest is like a mound or something that goes up and then turns down toward the school.

I should probably give you some info on where things are around school so you can see it in your brain otherwise you probably aren't gonna believe what happens next as I still don't even believe it really.

This cross country woods small mound area is way off across a wide green grass field to the west of the school. There's a small parking lot for cars of teachers on that side of school too. The main parking lot is in front of the school on the south side. That's where all the kids park. That's where the main entrance is too. There's lots of soccer fields and football fields and stuff on the far north side behind the school. There's parking lots there too but you can't get there straight from the other parking lots and the front entrance. You hafta come in by another entrance just for that sports stuff and you can't get all the way to the school from there anyway.

So I make the top of the mound in the middle of the woods and I stop. It's pretty sunny but also part shady there on top and I look through the trees. The trees are moving just a bit in the little wind. I look all around down toward the school and I see and hear alotta normal things. I look at the soccer fields first. I bend down somewhat and sure enough I see the girls in their purple shorts and white shirts with the little circle satellite pictures on em. I hear faint shouting from down there and some whistles blowing. There's already lots of teacher cars in the teacher parking lot and a few cars coming into the student parking lot too.

That's about it for the normal things. The rest is not so normal. There's Sherlock Interpol cars flashing their lights parked pretty much everywhere. There's like a hundred of em for true real. The whole front entrance is blocked off by em and they have like a checkpoint thing set up there stopping and talking to cars as they come in. There's a line of parked Sherlock Interpol cars in the teacher lot too on this side between me and the school. I see about ten more cop cars too way over by the soccer fields at the edge of the football stadium parking lot. I think it looks like a China Prison Camp or something but I'm sure Cass is happy about it.

So I start walking down the trails of the mound through the trees toward the teacher parking lot field area. The last big part of the trails kinda opens up at the edge of the woods and it's pretty steep so you gotta be careful coming down it. I was always happy about it being here for cross country causa it meant you got this hard part outta the way first. I stop just at the top of it and the path here is real more torn up more than I remember it.

And then I see it. It's tire tracks really and I think for a sec that some of the circus baboons have been tearing up here in their trucks again. Then I see the other thing and my heart pumps right outta my body I swear to god. To my right there is a big thicket of bushes between two fat trees only it's way more thick than I remember it. True I see it in the thicket and know it right away. The crappy ole white van is parked in there and covered up by alotta torn off branches and leaves and things for camo.

Goddamn Goat Ed never did drive away at all but came straight here last night and just hid himself out. The Sherlock Interpols are looking in every damn other state except here at school the idiots. I freeze for a minute and then I do something that I'm still not sure why I did it. I walk acoupla steps closer to the van. I just want to see or something or make sure. But if I could go back I'd just run right from there and straight down to Cass on the soccer field. But I bet if I did it that way something even worse coulda happened who knows with the Third Fig Newton Law working.

So I bend down a little bit to look and I see Goat Ed kinda asleep right there behind the steering wheel. His eyes are closed anyway and his face is redder than you can imagine and wet and scratched some too. He's been crying for sure. And right then he wakes up or opens his eyes and he stares right at me. He bends his head over looking through the thickets looking right at me.

"You OK Goat Ed?" I have no idea why I say it but I say it without thinking.

He looks at me super angry and super sad at the same time and I see he's kinda crying still. Then he shoves his hand outta the window and shows me this little black box with some wires coming outta it and a light on it.

"You stay right there Joker." His voice is cracking bad causa he's really crying now.

Now I have no ideas in my head what to do at all but my mouth just goes on it's own and all I really think about is Cass and how she's gonna be and how I wasn't ever gonna see her again. But my mouth talks anyway while I'm thinking about Cass. "I'm sorry what happened to your dad."

Now this is a true stupid thing to say as it breaks out his crying all worse and I realize it is causa he doesn't know nothing about his dad and he is just finding out. That's when he starts up the van and floors it and the big ole crappy white thing smashes outta the thicket at me. I put my hands up to catch it or something and he slams on the breaks and right before the van's gonna run me over and kill me it slides across the dirt and barely hits my hands with the lightest touch.

I slip backwards down the steep trail some and he leans out the window then all crying but he gathers himself some and wipes off his mouth with his sleeve and says, "Get yourself onto school now Joker. Go slow. I'm coming with."

"OK OK Ed." I have my hands in the air still trying to catch the van if it comes at me. He revs up the engine fierce and I turn and stumble down the path before he runs me over. I practically fall the whole way down the path it's so steep and Goat Ed waits til I'm nearly at the bottom then he eases the van onto the steepest part of the path. The van slides sideways down a bit and he locks up the breaks and I can't believe he doesn't roll it coming down and I can't see at all how he got the thing up there in the first place. It musta taken alotta tries and that's why it's all tore up.

The van comes at me sliding pretty fast near the bottom. I run out from under the last trees onto the green grass field after and Goat Ed shouts Joker from the van. I freeze there and the van kinda bounces onto the grass and comes to a stop right in front of me. I smell the grass some but real quick it's covered up by the dirty ole van exhaust and some other bad egg smell I don't recognize.

"Get on Joker. Slow," he says almost calm now but still crying a little.

I turn and start to walk across the big bumpy grass field toward the teacher's parking lot. The van creeps along behind me and Goat Ed guns the engine every now and then which sends my heart pumping outta my body each time.

No one sees us coming for like a billion years I swear and we just crawl along like snails. I tell myself it's now time for a true dealin plan but I have nothing coming in my brain now except Cass. I look at the soccer field trying to see her. I can't even tell which one is her out there really but I pick out one that think might be her and I hope it's her but I don't know it's too far.

Then they musta saw the van causa the sirens started blaring and the Sherlock Interpols started tearing in from everywhere into the teacher's parking lot area in their blaring cars.

There are like forty of em now all lining up between me and the school in their blaring cars and Goat Ed pushes me towards em slow and steady. There's no way he's gonna be able to get through em to the school I think which is good but not so good for me. And bad for alotta the Sherlock Interpols too. True bad for me and everybody if he blows this thing up on us.

The siren cars blaring creep around on both sides of us now too but then Goat Ed screams something loud and terrible outta the van window and that sorta stops em in a sorta horse shoe thing around us. There is a guy saying something on a megaphone thing but my heart is pumping so loud I can't hear it. Then Goat Ed screams back like a animal dying and his face is all redder and I don't understand anything he says but at least the megaphone goes quiet for a while after that.

Then we're only about fifty feet left to go to the line of blaring cars and I see one of the soccer players running now across the far field this way and I know it's Cass for sure causa she's the only one running this way. It wasn't the one I thought was her was before but now I'm glad at least I can see her the right one at least one more time for sure and I start to cry a little bit then.

Then the van stops kinda creaking in the field behind me. I don't look back causa I think the worst is coming so I just keep looking at Cass running. Then I hear Goat Ed's voice. It's pretty quiet now and low and growling but not like an animal anymore, "Go ahead Joker. Get yourself onto school," he says it real quiet so only I hear it and no one else.

I walk super slow away from the van and I see one of the Sherlock Interpols holding back Cass by the blaring cars and then she goes blurry in the tears and I wipe em away with the back of my hand real quick because I don't want my last look at her to be all blurred like that and then the explosion happens. I'm pretty near the cop cars already when it goes off and the last thing I see is the cops running out to me. Then I go all outta it like maybe I'm going to sleep or something.

If I try to remember what it was like before I went all asleep I think it was loud and hot really that's all I remember. Loud enough that it hurt in my brain. Then there's the noise and then I feel a bad pain on my face. That's really all I can remember though they did say I was awake most of the time all the way to the hospital. Cass says I was awake but all I said to her was "I can't hear anything" and acourse "*true*".

14

Grand Central Station obviously. The worst of that bad is over now and I'll tell you true right now that I did not die so you don't hafta wait forever to find out like some stupid stories. In fact it wasn't really close to me dying which may surprise you. Wait first things first I'll get to that more in a sec.

The bad pain on my face was my broken nose. That isn't from the explosion legally but from when I got knocked onto the ground. It was the ground that did that. The only real bad parts are my ears and some burns all over the back of my head. The backpack and books helped some so that part wasn't worse. The doctor types at the hospital said at first I might not get my hearing back at all Cass told me. But after acoupla days it started coming back. It's most of the way back now and I hear pretty good but the doctor types say that's probably going to be as good as it gets for me.

If it's OK I'll kinda take a Holton Bolton angle on the rest of this stuff as I'm sure you're done again with bad smashing stories for now. My nose is all blacked and blued and I hafta wear a stupid support across it for a while. My hair is burned off mostly at the back and the burned skin there is all caked up with scabs and stuff and I hafta wear a big head wrap on there. So here I am pretty all blacked and blued and still wearing my black arg pirate patch and my nose thing now and my head wrap and I look like a complete idiot acourse. Holton Bolton loves it though I can't get back to the hardware store til I get a lot better.

Holton Bolton comes to visit me at the hospital and then at Cass's after. It's weird having him at Cass's house. Kinda like taking a big ole pink pig to a palace or something. OK now some of the more serious stuff.

Luckily but still bad at least for Goat Ed I guess Goat Ed is the only one who died in the explosion. Turns out he planned it out that way. There were no nails in the van at all or sure I'd be true dead and so would alotta the Sherlock Interpols. They found the nails all dumped out a little way back in the woods from where he was hiding his van. He also dumped out alotta the fertilizer and whatnot that him and his dad had mixed up in the barrels. His dad wanted it so it would kill all the bad people at school he was so mad about. But Goat Ed pretty much changed it to kill himself.

Still it coulda killed a lot more easily and so they called it a legal terror attack and that sorta took everything up to the next level around here. First thing the school people and the local Sherlock Interpols were pretty much taken outta things from then on. That actually makes some sense if you think about it based on how bad they did things so far. True idiots acourse. So the governor pretty much shuts em all down and sends in the National Guard Armies as you might have guessed. Then the FBI Jacket Guys pour in all over too and they did their own Sherlock Interpol thing but at a higher level. Nobody knows who was in charge anymore exactly not even Cass's dad. But one thing's for sure it's not the school Principals and Supers or the Sherlock Local Interpols anymore.

School just stops that's all. We are close to finals anyway and summer is just a ways off so they decide to just shut it down for the rest of the year. *True dream come true.* Some kids think that anyway but not really causa everything that's happened. One thing that goes on is soccer though causa the girls are so close to state. They do go on to get it after all in the end too so that is one great thing for Cass. It's also a pretty good thing for the whole town really. It gives everybody something to talk about which isn't bad. There is still a little bit of the bad blustering going around I hear but it's pretty quiet now. One thing about having a ton a FBI Jacket Guys and National Guard Armies crawling all over is that no one talks too loud or crazy around town.

I actually go to the soccer finals to watch Cass though my mom has to help me a lot as I'm still pretty broke some. Finals are at state college which makes it pretty fun for me and my mom causa it's kinda like our favorite town. The game is on this new soccer field they have there which has this new kinda really good looking bright green fake grass. Later Cass says it smells bad playing on it. Like old car tires. I tell Cass that I can't think of a much worse thing than making beautiful green grass but taking the real grass smell outta it. She says that's true. She's been saying that more now causa being around me.

Me and mom stay overnight in state college city after Cass wins states. She says it's a good time for me to just get away from our town for a bit. The next day after Cass does her real party with her team we all go to mom's favorite ole bar restaurant together. I should probably tell you the place is called *Dancers* so you can go there if you are ever in state college city. I know the name sounds stupid but the name is actually from way back when stuff like that wasn't stupid. We all have burgers together and mom has acoupla beers and she talks more than normal and talks to Cass a lot too which is weird. It's nice being there with Cass and mom even though I mostly just sit there while they talk.

Acourse the Dan Kenneth Rathers get more and more all over our town. This thing in our town is so bad that even the president mentions us in a kinda way when he's talking. This ends up forcing acoupla legal district people from our town outta their jobs. We get new legal district people after that and they work more with the FBI Jacket Guys on all the stuff that happened. One thing that came of this was that they actually legally charged Jeff and the other baboons for what they did in the shower with me.

Even though alotta time has passed I guess it wasn't too late for justice on em so they arrest Eric and Jamie and the other circus baboons too. They say it happened causa most of the Dan Kenneth Rathers were saying they oughta on TV. Whyever it was it makes me feel a little bit better about what happened. One thing that does not make me feel better at all is when they go to arrest Jeff he's gone. *True disappeared. True acourse.*

Cass is pretty worried about Jeff being gone. She says it was bad too when he was around but at least you could see him around then. Now having him disappeared makes it worse. Even though the Jeff thing is going on Cass and me still have some really good days right after states. She has a lot more time to spend with me but still not a ton of time causa she doesn't just let off of working on her soccer as you probably can guess.

She signs up for this camp on soccer at state college so she goes up there twice a week and stays all day. This camp is legally just for people on the state college team but they let Cass into it even though she hasn't legally signed up for state college yet anyway. I guess they really want her to sign up that's all. She also does sports things in our town on the other days but it's less than before.

I start running with Cass on the other mornings when she doesn't go to state college. Well true I don't run with her the whole time but I start out with her each day anyway. She runs for a long time but she starts out slow with me and calls it her warming up. Then when I start to get tired out she dusts me up and takes off and disappears ahead and then comes back around and catches me right before the end. It's fun anyway for me causa it reminds me of cross country and gets me back up on some running.

Then in the evenings and nights we have alotta time together. We do all sorta things together and I'm not gonna tell you all of em but I'll tell you a couple. I'll tell you em causa it means some things were changing for us even though I didn't know it then.

Anyway I tell Cass about my walk into the school the day I was blown up as I forgot it mostly for a while but then it comes back and I told Cass that it was actually a pretty nice walk despite me being blown up at the end. I tell her we might wanna make the walk together sometime for her to see it. She says it's kinda morbid or something but she eventually agrees to it. Then we end up doing the walk on a Wednesday I think or whatever day she isn't at state college.

We have dinner early so we can get out and back before it's dark. Cass is serious on that so we make plans on it and time it right. It's a hot afternoon and sunny. I think summer is on already for real or at least close. There is mowers buzzing kinda quiet as always far off when we start out. Cass dingers the Miller's door and asks if we can cut through the woods and the Miller lady stares at me for acoupla hours it seems but says sure.

The ground is more dried up in the woods than I remember from the day I was exploded. But it still smells really good for a woods and I hold Cass's hand as we walk and I tell her about the smell. She agrees the smell is true and we laugh at her saying true without even thinking about it.

We cross over the Farm Road and the Rambo Fence and we walk slow holding our hands together with our arms stretched out between us. This kinda knocks the long yellow grass down between us as we go. We go real slow and I see that Cass is looking at the long dry grass and at the sky but not at all at me. She looks kinda serious and I ask her about what she's thinking. She says she doesn't know for sure. She says it's nice here though and I say true to it and we walk forever through the grass.

We decide to stop before we go to the fish pond. We just sit down in the grass that's all. Well first we walk around on it smashing it down in a little spot for us to sit. We sit there kissing for a long time but not too long so we don't get back after dark. And then we do a real long and slow Shake Spear Love Poem. I know I said I was done telling you about em but this one was kinda different so I should say it. I didn't know at the time what it meant at all or that it was even different really but now I know. All I can say is that it's really long and slow and quiet and Cass is a little different than before. She is less excited about it and more serious that's all. Acourse I'm still just as excited and everything and I don't know anything at the time.

We walk more through the grass after and take the short way around the Fish Pond and then we spend a little while at the ole McKenzie Dead Cement Factory. We look in through the broken windows everywhere and it's spooky somewhat. I say we should go in and poke around. Cass says no and it's a good thing we didn't I think. Finally we think we hear a banging somewhere inside there and this scares the shit outta both of us so we bolt outta there. We don't go anywhere near the mound woods by the school causa I don't really want to as you can imagine.

I get Cass back out to the Schmidt farm too a few more times to watch the sunset over all the sod grass. We sit for an hour sometimes or more in the car parked at our little patch in the woods across the street. We watch the trucks dusting up the little roads and spraying and sometimes the sprinklers come on for watering the grass. This is really nice if the sun is real low causa the water kinda sparkles in the sunlight. We listen to Cass's music quiet too like usual and talk and kiss too.

We did one other thing during this time that I wanna tell you about too. I drive Cass up to state college for her soccer camp and I sit in the stands and watch her all day and eat my lunch in a bag on the metal bleachers. I got the idea for what we did next when I take a leak in the stadium shitters. When I'm washing my hands I also wash my face off some with cold water like I like to do sometimes. I'm drying my face with a hard brown paper thing and then I look at myself in the mirror and I look a lot different. I mean my arg pirate patch is gone now and my nose thing is off and my head bandage is gone. But the skin around my eyes is still kinda bruised and darker and there are some small scars all around my face. Anyway I think I look like a different person or at least an older person.

After the day camp I tell Cass about what I saw in the mirror and she says it's true. I do look different. Then I tell her I made a small plan on going to Dancers for a burger with her and ordering a beer to see if I can get it. She says I'm crazy causa I go there all the time and they know me. I tell her that they are all kinda super old and dumb there and they don't know me for shit at all. She tells me that I don't look that old even with my face all smashed. I say we should try anyway and she stares at me forever before smiling really big and saying OK OK.

Well we are nervous as hell and giddy too but you will not believe it Cass is a cool customer or whatever during it. I order the beer right off but kinda mess it up causa I say it and then stutter right during asking. The old lady taking the order doesn't say a thing at all but just asks what I want to eat. So then Cass orders a beer too after she orders her burger which wasn't part of the plan at all. The old lady looks at her for an extra second but says OK to it and walks away.

We laugh but real quiet causa we don't want the lady to hear and decide we're just kids. We have two beers each and eat our burgers. We are pretty excited for the rest of the night probably causa adrenaline from our plan working but also causa the beers. We hafta wait awhile and walk around state college some before we drive back to our town.

15

OK OK something happens next. It's not a bad Grand Central Station thing but it's still kinda bad in a small or different kinda way. I'm not going to make up a new trick for it or anything but if I hafta describe it I'll say it's sorta like a small train leaving the station. It's just a small thing really but still a little bad and when you look back on it later it's really a big thing. The kinda thing you remember for a long time anyway.

I know I didn't say that good enough for you to get what I mean exactly but Mrs. H. says I should just leave it that it's good enough and you will know by what comes next what I'm talking about.

So I notice Cass being a little more serious and not looking at me like when I just told you about in the tall grass. Well as you probably guessed already it comes out right after that. We're in her basement one night. We're down there to watch a movie but before it we're just lying all tangled up on the couch kissing and talking. We do that for like an hour and we never really get around to starting a movie and this is when she says it.

"Joseph." Now she looks right at me with those serious eyes. I'm stupid as I said before but even I know that only bad stuff comes out right then. But I say nothing back at all causa I was trying to get ahead and think about what was coming. So she eventually just goes on, "You know I love you right Joseph?"

Acourse I am still pretty stupid and don't get to what's coming at all so I just say what I always say, "True Cass."

"I have to pick my school now Joseph. I'm running out of time." She is pretty calm and cool but still she looks at me like that with those serious eyes while she talks.

"True Cass. I think you should pick state college. I can come up then and we can go to dates at Dancers." I say it with a pretty happy voice and I am still pretty stupid about what is going on at that point which I'm sure makes Cass believe even more in what she needs to do to me.

"I was thinking that it might be better for me to go out East instead Joseph." She talks way too slow like she's talking to a little kid or a foreign person and then and I start to get it a bit.

"True no way Cass." I feel a little desperate about it. I'm kinda scared in my stomach pit. Kinda sick actually. I feel really like I hafta puke some.

"I think it may be for the best Joseph." She sees me twisting up I'm sure right before her and I actually kinda sit up sorta rough at this point but she keeps going on causa really what else can she do at that point.

"You're very young Joseph. That's one of the things I love about you the most. The whole world is new to you. But you're also old for your age and you are pretty good at seeing the world for how it really is."

"That's true Cass. But I don't..." She cuts me right off acourse causa she's already going.

"This thing between us is different for you and me." She kinda pauses and I wanna yell or something at her but she kinda shuts me up with her eyes and goes on. "Now I don't know which way of seeing it is really true Joseph, as you like to say. But it is true that I see this differently than you because I've done it a few times already. It will be different for you too when you've done it a few more times too Joseph."

"True but what if I don't wanna to do it a few more times. What if I wanna do just this one?' My voice is mad and also cracking just a little bit which makes me think of Goat Ed for a second which is weird.

"Joseph it doesn't usually work like that," she says it pretty quiet but pretty firm.

"We can make it work like that Cass. True we can." I kinda plead legally the way I do but I also kinda know already that I am losing my legal case against her.

"It's possible Joseph. That's true. I mean if anyone can do it you can do it. You've been through a lot already and I'm so proud of you for it." She starts to sound like my mom and that makes me feel different about her for a sec but I kinda push that outta my mind. She goes on while I work that out in my head. "Joseph, I was thinking it might be best for us to make a clean break when I go to college. That will save us....that will save you....the true bad feelings of disappointment later on."

That kinda gets me mad causa she is using my own words against me. True I gotta admit I start to cry then some but here is what I do anyway. It's quiet for a real long time and I wipe my face all up. I am thinking on a plan. I guess you can even say I was dealin a little bit just then. But I'm not working too hard on it. It's just happening. But some kinda plan does come to me.

"True Cass anything is possible. You even said it yourself." I lean in and kiss her and that was not really part of my dealin plans but I just do it. Maybe it's what really made it work. "I'm not afraid of my broken heart Cass. I've got everything else broken on me now and I'm not afraid of it. If you gotta break it or if it somehow just breaks later I'll be OK Cass. True I'll be OK. True I won't blame you Cass."

"But Joseph..." I kinda work my plan and I'm a little excited about it even the way I get about plans. I don't want to let her go til I get most or all of it out so I just go on and cut her off.

"If you wanna break it now Cass that's OK do it. If it's true how you feel then do it. If you just wanna protect me causa you think you'll break it later then don't do it Cass. True don't do it causa anything is possible as you said. If it happens it happens. True OK I promise. But just let it happen when it happens."

That gets her a bit but not all the way. I think she's pretty much made up her mind about it before we even started talking. But I kinda got her turned a little causa my dealin. We sit there staring at each other like true idiots for like an hour then.

"Oh Joseph. I don't know." Her eyes were nice then and not serious at all but her shoulders were hunched down a little bit.

"I'll go home now Cass. I mean back to my true house. You think on it. I'll stay away I promise. You think on it til you are sure and then you call me. I'll even answer the phone I promise."

"Ok Joseph." She nods and I see she is true not sure anymore. I give Cass one more kiss and then I get up and go outta there and go back to my true house just like I said. I sleep at my house alone for the first time in like a billion years.

16

The phone rings twice the next day and I actually answer it both times acourse hoping it's Cass but it's just those Dan Kenneth Rathers so I hang up on em. My mom sees me answer the phone one time and she stands there staring at me like I'm a zombie or something. She asks me if everything is OK with Cass and I just say I don't know for sure yet but I will know soon enough. She looks at me worse than she did even when I was in the hospital but she doesn't say anything and just lets me alone.

I go outside to sorta get away from the phone for the rest of the day. But I still listen into the house mostly as I do things anyway. I tune up the crappy ole mower for a while causa the yard is like a jungle and needs cutting. But after I get it all tuned up I don't even start it causa I don't want to miss the phone if it rings out inside. But acourse it never rings the rest of the day.

That night I can't take it waiting. Then I really wish I didn't tell Cass I'd stay away with a promise and I don't think I'll be able to do it another night. So I get a plan on that and I call up Pup and he says sure come over and I get a whole bunch of beers and go over to his house. Pete is there and Hokey too and it's just like old times except there is a new guy there named Ted who keeps looking at me sideways. I can't tell if he is scared of me or mad at me or if it's just causa my face is all smashed up but eventually I get from the way that Pup is talking that he is kinda my replacement in the gang. Maybe he is worried that I am back and he'll get kicked out or something or maybe he wants to kick me out. Anyway I keep my eye on him causa I really can't get another smashing as you can imagine.

There is also acoupla the usual girls there hanging onto Pup and Hokey some. Nicky and Di. Not the Di from the riots but a different Di. These two girls get to asking me alotta questions about Cass the way girls do that about other girls and I answer em true but very short and I don't get into much of what is going on. I mean the whole reason to be there is to not think about it. They acourse see me kinda bothered by it and keep going after me like piranha fishes in blooded waters or something til Pup finally tells em to let me alone. Pup says that I've practically been killed like three times already and to give me a break.

After that it's pretty good and we have a pretty big fire in Pup's woods and I just lay there next to the fire drinking beers til practically morning. Acourse as morning comes on I start thinking about Cass all over again causa I can't help it so I decide to head home.

Ted is passed out and the girls are gone by then but Pup and Hokey say bye to me and tell me to come back later this week again. I promise em but I never did it.

OK I shouldn't a drove home at all as you can imagine. My mom says it to me later but she says it a lot more quiet than I expected. I guess she thinks like Pup that when a guy almost gets killed a few times then he gets a break. Anyway nothing too bad happened except I ran over our mailbox and knocked out one of the headlights on the crappy ole Ford Taurus and left the front door open when I went in.

My mom wakes me up later with a big water and a coffee which is strange. She tells me that someone is here to see me. Before she goes out though she tells me never to drink and drive and then tells me about how I ran over the mailbox and how I smashed the headlight on her crappy ole Ford Taurus and how I need to fix the headlight. I promise her I'll fix it all today and I say I won't drink and drive again.

She says she already fixed the mailbox but that it would be nice if I did the headlight causa she didn't want to get pulled over driving from work some night. I don't really believe what she said about fixing the mailbox but we'll see. Then she leaves and in comes Cass if you can believe it.

"Joseph this is exactly the sort of thing you can't do when you're sad or mad at me," Cass says it as she sits down at my bed and I try to figure out what it means for us but I have a hard time especially causa my head hurts.

"If we're going to be together, then you've got to promise me you'll be more grown up about it if we have trouble." She sorta touches my head as she says it and I take a big ole swig of the coffee. It's sweet as hell causa that's how my mom takes it. Then I finally figure it out what Cass is saying and I am super happy as you can imagine.

"True we're gonna be together still Cass?" I say it almost like a kid on Christmas but I try to act more grownup causa what she just said.

"True let's give it the old college try Joseph." She smiles a really big smile at me and kisses me and most of that sorta serious look she had on her face recently is now gone but not all of it.

"True you're going out east still Cass?" This one is kinda a big question so I look at her kinda crazy.

"False Joseph. I'm going to state. I've got my papers in the car and I'm going to drive them up today because they're a little past the deadline already. Do you want to come with me?" She grabs my coffee this time and takes a big drink off of it herself.

"True yes Cass. That's great. I got some small plans about it if you want to hear em." I take my coffee back and start to get up.

"Tell me on the way up Joseph. I want to get back before dark." Cass takes my coffee and tells me to get dressed quick.

17

True we're getting on toward the end of the story. Also true there is another pretty big Grand Central Station coming up before it's over sorry to hafta tell you if you are tired a hearing it. But really at this point telling you Grand Central Station doesn't work anymore. You're just gonna hafta get through it or quit. That's all. It's like skipping stupid Romeo on Juliet killing theirselves or something. Yeah sure it's hard and Grand Central Station but it's not really a true story at all if you skip it. I mean you can't even legally say you read a Shake Spear Love Poem if you skip those parts.

The ride up to state in the car is abouta nice a ride as I ever had. The sun shines hot and we have the windows down the whole way even on the highway. Cass says no to the AC when I ask about it so we just let the wind howl and bluster all into the car. We shout right over it when we talk the first part of the ride but then later we just blast some music she wants to listen to. She plays some kinda new kid's dance music. It's weird and everything but I like it some still. Like I said she listens to all kinda music. Blasting music and going fast in a car with the windows down and the sun all around is a pretty good way to get to state college.

I shout out to her over the blustering winds about my plans that I have been dealin up. I tell her that I hafta go into school soon to talk to a counsel person anyway causa all that's happened to me. I am going to ask the counsel person about summer classes and this thing about early graduation that you can sign up for that Pup's girl Nicky told me all about around the fire. Her cousin did it and skipped his senior year and went away to the University of Berkley Beach instead.

Cass tells me it's a great plan and a great goal but not to get upset if I can't do it. That it will be very hard. True I will do it for sure I tell her.

I tell Cass I am a little nervous for her papers being late at state college. What if they don't take em? She tells me not to worry causa they gave her a athletic type scholarship already and special type exemption or something like that.

We get there and back to state college in no time. We even have lunch at Dancers but we don't try the beer thing again causa I just had like a billion of em and ran over my mailbox last night.

When we get back it wasn't even dinner time yet so I have Cass drop me off at my house so I can fix my mom's crappy ole Ford Taurus headlight. I asked Cass if I can pick her up and take her out to the Schmidt's later to look at the sunset and the sod grass after dinner. To sorta celebrate our not breaking up yet anyway. She says OK.

I take my mom's car over to the parts store and get what I need there and I even stop into Holton Bolton's hardware store and chat with him for a little bit. I'm kinda over excited about what happened with Cass as you can imagine and I need to tell someone about it. Holton doesn't get it at all but it's good for me to talk about it anyway. I tell him about how we are going to the Schmidt's to watch the sunset and everything.

This gets Holton Bolton asking about Goat Ed again and I kinda hafta go over it again with him about how Cass and I Sherlock Interpoled it. Now he is either confused or maybe sad about Goat Ed so I get outta there causa I don't wanna lose the good feelings I'm having about the Cass thing.

I get my mom's crappy ole Ford Taurus light fixed finally but it takes me forever. It's getting on close to dark so I hafta speed some over to Cass's to get her before sunset. This makes me nervous and a little sick feeling causa it's just like last night when I was driving home and something bad coulda happened from doing that.

I get Cass and she jumps into the car and she says she has some special music picked out for us to listen to at the Schmidt's tonight. I say great and we go out to the River Road pretty fast and make it to our pine woods patch just in time for the sun to go down.

OK so right away she plays this song called Joker that is pretty old. I tell her acourse I know it from the oldies radio causa everybody's always called me Joker even when I was a kid. Well instead of listening to the music quiet like normal we turn it way up and go through it acoupla times in a row singing along with it real loud. I mean Goat Ed and his dad are dead now anyway and we're not Sherlock Interpoling anything so we don't hafta be quiet.

The sun goes all the way down and it's true dark out and the Joker song starts finishing off the last time and just then a big ole pickup truck comes roaring past. There are a bunch of guys in the front and back part of the truck and they're screaming and they throw a beer can out the window at our car. Cass turns the radio off and we watch the truck speed loud away down the River Road. It's real quiet and dark in our car then and Cass says, "Joseph, that wasn't Jeff's truck was it?"

"Dunno Cass. I don't think so. But it's pretty dark. Wanna get outta here?" I watch the red truck tail lights get smaller way up on the River Road and the rumbling noise of the truck gets quieter. Then the truck makes a left turn off the river road away from the river up on the hill where the road is all new from just being widened. We watch the lights disappear into the trees.

"Yeah Joseph. Let's go," Cass says sounding nervous. "Do you want me to drive? I might see better in the dark."

"No I'll do it Cass." I'm nervous a bit too and I just wanna get going. We were both still staring at the turn off in the trees up on the hill on the river road.

I pull out onto the River Road and speed up pretty quick as fast as the crappy ole Ford Taurus will get going up the hill. "I'll go straight out the River Road Cass OK?" If it was normal we'd turn off where the truck turned off into the trees to get back to Cass's house.

Cass says OK and she puts on her seatbelt. I'm still pretty nervous and trying to watch the road careful so I don't put on my seatbelt which is a big mistake. I speed up pretty good as we climb up the long hill on the River Road. The pavement there is all new and true black with some shining spots all over it. The yellow lines in the middle and the white ones on the sides are bright as hell and fresh painted which I'm glad for so I can see em in the dark.

There is a pretty big new culvert type thing under the hill of the new part of the River Road that opens up onto the river and there is a big long slope of real fresh cut looking big rocks that runs steep all the way down to the water. Good for us there is a bright shiny new rail all along that side of the road so I don't drive over the edge into the river causa I can't see good at night.

We make it the road where the truck turned into the woods and we both look down it stretching our necks and Cass practically leans all the way over me looking. We don't see any lights. It's not surprising though really causa that turnoff road only goes abouta half mile before it curves into some trees so you can't really see anything in there.

"You see anything Cass?" I ask her nervous as hell still watching the road careful.

"No Joseph." She bends her neck around toward the back to look down road again. Then she yells, "There!"

My heart pumps practically outta my body and I swerve the car kinda violent and it screeches on the road but I get it back straight before we run into the bright shiny new rail. Then I see the headlights flashing on the turnoff road too and they're coming faster than anything back down the road toward us. I stomp on the gas all the way down to the floor and the crappy ole Ford Taurus whines pretty bad but it doesn't go much faster as we get up towards the top part of the hill. Just as we are getting to the top part of the hill I see the truck turn really wild onto the River Road behind us. There are screeches from the truck sliding around the corner and I hear a crash from the truck swiping the bright shiny new rail and I think for a second the truck's gonna roll right over the edge but it comes off the rail and speeds up the road again behind us.

"You got your phone Cass?" I kinda yell at her and look at her for a second. She holds onto the dashboard with both hands and looks scared as hell as you can imagine. I am too acourse.

"No Joseph. I didn't bring it." She is true scared as hell and I think to myself for a sec if we get out of this I'm getting a phone acourse even if I don't like em.

"Hold on!" I yell louder this time.

I am glad for the downhill part coming but the crappy ole Ford Taurus only picks it up a little as we start down. I hear the rumbling and the screeching of the truck behind us and I think I can hear the screaming of the guys too. It's Jeff I think causa he's a big ole truck baboon and I think that beast will be on us in about two more seconds. And sure enough the headlights come over the crest of the hill behind us right away. In the mirror I see acoupla guys at least standing in the back part of the truck and they're shaking around pretty bad back there and holding on for their lives and screaming and hollering.

Cass turns around in her seat and watches em too. "Faster Joseph"

"True faster Cass. They're tearing at us Cass." That was about all I get out when they smash right into the back of the crappy ole Ford Taurus coming down the hill of the River Road.

The crappy ole Ford Taurus screams across the pavement turning sideways and we mighta twirled once all the way around or two I don't know but then my side of the car tips up off the road and I know we are in bad trouble then. The car rolls right off the road and over the bright shiny new rail and it slams down onto the big fresh cut rock that are sloping down to the river. I feel a bad sharp pain on my forehead. There's scraping metal and smashing and tearing. We probably turn four times over on the rocks or more but I don't know. And then everything stops turning and everything goes quiet except some creaking noises and some hissing.

I open up my eyes and we're sitting upright on the rocks like we mighta drove nice and easy down the slope and parked partways down. Everything is red as hell even the night sky and there is glass everywhere in my lap and all around on the dash and in the front seat.

"Joseph!" I hear Cass yelling at me and then I see her kneeling on the seat next to me. She looks OK except she was dusty and everything is red as hell.

"You OK Cass?" I manage but it sounds kinda echoey.

"I'm fine Joseph. My airbag went off but yours didn't. You're cut pretty bad Joseph. Damn we should have taken my car!" She sounds bad nervous and I feel her touching around my forehead all gentle. "True they wouldn't a caught us in your car Cass." I kinda drop my head back and close my eyes and then I feel kinda tired and I think for a sec if there were any parts in the crappy ole Ford Taurus book about making em go faster but I can't remember.

Then I hear Cass scream and I open my eyes and some asshole circus baboon named Tom and some other guy are pulling Cass right outta the window. Then I turn my head the other way and there's Jeff. He's standing with his shirt off right at my window. I open my mouth to say something to the true baboon but right then he hits me in the face. That's the kinda guy Jeff is he'll hit someone that's practically dead already.

Then Jeff pulls me right outta the window too. I hit my head bad on the door as I come out and I scream at Jeff but he just keeps pulling. That's when I see his truck above. He drove it right through the bright shiny new rail and parked it on the rocks and the lights are shining right down on us and I can hear it rumbling. The doors are open and I think for a sec I see a big pink face sitting in the middle of the front seat.

Jeff drags me over the rocks and then throws me down. I hit my head good on the rocks and then I hear Cass screaming. I look around for the screaming and everything is still red but I see Cass about ten feet away on the rocks. There are three guys holding her down and one is Tom for sure but I can't see the other two. Must be Richy I think and somebody else and then I see em tear her shirt right off of her and she screams again. I try to lift my head to say something but right then Jeff kicks me right in the side.

Jeff yells something at me and then I roll onto my side on the rocks toward Cass and I see Cass's shirt and bra are both torn all off and they're pulling her pants down too and then they tear her underwear off too. She's mostly naked with her pants down around her legs and I see everything. I see Tom put his hand between her legs and she screams again. Then I pick up my head and scream for the fucking baboons to let her alone and it's a good thing I move my head then causa right as I scream Jeff drops a giant rock down with both hands where my head was. The rock mostly misses me but hits me sorta on the very top part of my head and my head bounces down onto another rock below it. Then everything goes pretty black.

I open my eyes and everything is still red but I see Cass kneeling right over me. She holds her torn up shirt at her front and she has her jeans all back on again. She's has a big cut on her lip and she was pretty much yelling at me, "Joseph! Joseph!"

"I'm here Cass. True I'm here," I say it kinda garbled up and she cries like mad and she hugs me around the head which kinda hurts and I groan and she loosens up some. Her hands are all covered in blood from where she been holding onto my head.

"Someone stopped Joseph. They called the police Joseph. They're coming. An ambulance will be here soon." She sounds crazy and she is all covered in blood and she gently wipes my cheeks with her bloody hands.

"Where's Jeff Cass?" I say suddenly scared as hell again.

Cass lifts her head and motions up with her chin and then she points a bloody finger too, "He's there Joseph. He's dead."

I kinda turn my head which doesn't really want to move and I see Jeff laying flat out and limp on the rocks with his bare chest facing up at the sky and his arms spread out and tangled beside him. I only kinda see his face which is turned to the side and his head is all bloody and the part of his face I can see is all red.

That's when I see Holton sitting on the rock just past where Jeff was laying. He has a big ole black eye and puffy lips and he's crying. Not true blubbering but crying real quiet and he has his knees pulled up against his chest and he is rocking kinda back and forth.

"True Holton?" I say not really knowing what's happened yet.

"True Holton Joseph. He did it. He hit Jeff in the head with a rock otherwise Jeff would have killed you." She looks at me and she's sorta calmed down.

Suddenly I remember Tom and Richy, "Did they rape you Cass?"

"No Joseph. But they would have if it wasn't for Holton. Tom and Rich and Wes ran off as soon as Holton hit Jeff with the rock." She wipes my cheek again which was just spreading the blood around and then she looks nervous again, "Joseph!"

"I'm tired Cass," I say to her and close my eyes.

"Hold on Joseph," she says quiet to me.

"True Cass," I whisper back.

18

So you probably guessed it that I wasn't gonna get to the end of my story without getting smashed at least one more time. That was just sorta the way it was going.

Well again I lived this time though my head was smashed pretty bad. The doctor types say it was not the rock that Jeff hit me with that really did it but the other one I bounced off of that did it. That made my brain swell up inside my skull and they thought that it was gonna make me brain dead. But it didn't obviously and the swelling started down right before they were gonna cut some of my head off to make more room for more swelling. Which is good causa I get to keep my whole head the way it is.

Cass is OK too I mean for a person who got partway raped. Later we joke that it's one thing that we both have in common getting partway raped but it takes a while before it's true funny. Everything else is just cuts and bruises for her which is true lucky.

Holton as you mighta guessed it got his big ole black eye causa Jeff and the angry baboons beat em up pretty good. They grabbed him from his house and he went along fine til they said they were coming for me. Then he said he wanted to go home so they hit him in the face til he told em I was probably at the Schmidt's with Cass. He just sat blubbering in Jeff's truck til he saw what they were gonna do with us and then he gets out and picks up a big ole rock and cracks Jeff's head open with it. Jeff never saw it coming and he died of it right away the doctor types say. True good for Jeff. *True thanks to Holton.*

Holton's cuts and bruises healed up OK but his brains were a little more shook up than they were before and they were shook up pretty good already as you know. I did go back once to visit him at the hardware store and we talked for a long time but it was different. He didn't laugh at my jokes at all and he was a lot more nervous about everything. At least he has the hardware store and that will give him something to do for probably the rest of his life.

How Jeff stayed hidden with his truck from the FBI Jacket Guys no one knew for sure for a long time til someone discovered some of his stuff inside the ole McKenzie Dead Cement Factory. I guess he drove his truck right in there and holed up and snuck around stealing stuff he needed. Then one night I guess he just comes out and tracks down Tom and Rich and Wes with his plan to get me. At least that's what the guys said in court. They mighta been lying who knows. Looks like even the FBI Jacket Guys can be true stupid too. Tom and Rich and Wes got legally put in jail for a long time for sex assault and attempting a murder on us. True they might get out later but they'll be really old. My mom says enough already of our town after that and she moves us to state college city. We rent an apartment there and sell our house in our town which takes a long time acourse causa people say it's haunted or spooked or something stupid like that. This is perfect for me as you can imagine since it's just where I want to be anyway causa Cass. My plans for early graduation are kinda screwed up causa my swollen brains. First I hafta go back and get alotta my speech and stuff like that fixed up before I can start on my regular classes not to mention my side classes and everything.

But I do get it all fixed up. They test me regular and now some of my speech and things like that are even higher than where it was at before as I was saying way back when we started this thing.

Mrs. H. drives up to our apartment twice a week and helps me with it some. I know it sounds like a lot but she actually lives really close to state college city and she just drives a long way every day to be a teacher in my old school. Mrs. H says I've been through alotta trials now and I somehow got off on every one of em. I guess she's right.

So I do graduate early but it's only part way through my senior year. I take lots of extra classes along the way to do it. I take some college classes too while I'm still finishing high school but not at state college at a community college where they have this thing for kids like me to take classes.

After that I do go on to state college. I don't hafta worry at all about paying for it causa I got paid for this story as you might have guessed. It isn't a billion dollars but it's just enough for school and enough for some other things like a trip to Paris for Cass and me. That's in the future some just after this story ends so I can't really tell you about it. Mrs. H. says that it's causa I never talked to any Dan Kenneth Rathers that I got some money for this story. Everyone wanted to hear my part of it causa I was quiet on it the whole time. I guess in the end by not dealin I ended up actually dealin though I didn't even know it.

Some kinda important stuff does actually happen between Cass and me soon later on but I'm not gonna tell you about it in here. That's a different story and I don't want to ruin this story by telling it in here. This story has to be just the way it is. *True that's how it was then.* Maybe I'll tell you about it later.

ABOUT THE AUTHOR

Jacob Heric (1975 – Kinda Soon) was born in Battle Creek, Michigan. He grew up in Wisconsin and studied literature at the great state University of Wisconsin at Madison. Studying literature was a bad idea and it nearly ruined any prospect of writing for him but he eventually recovered enough to record this chronicle as well as *Dew of Heaven* and *A Robin in the Springtime* (forthcoming titles from True Joker Company publications).

www.ingramcontent.com/pod-product-compliance
Lightning Source LLC
Chambersburg PA
CBHW021204130626
46554CB00005B/1977